To: Sara
Share the magic!

MW01700968

Magic Academy

Book 1

The Fire Test

E.R. Ross

by E.R. Ross

Superstorm Productions, LLC

Superstorm Productions

Other Works by E.R. Ross:

Magic Academy Series

Book One: **The Fire Test**
Book Two: **Murder at Seagrove**

Coming Soon:

Book Three: **Race to Red Skull**

Cover Design by Phatpuppy Art
Font/logo graphic design by Eden Crane

First American Edition Published in 2015 by Superstorm Productions, LLC
ISBN 978-1-941994-14-6

Magic Academy Book 1: The Fire Test

Website address: superstormproductions.wordpress.com
Rights & requests & fan mail & hate mail & "meh" mail:
superstormproductions@gmail.com

Many thanks to my family and friends
who support me writing about
fire breathing lizards
and labyrinths
and love
and other stuff and things.

Chapter One
Goodbye

This was a day of wall jumping! Of cloud racing! Of new sights and stranger-friends and new magical abilities finally within her reach.

Today Lace Labrencias was on her way to Magic Academy. She pursed her lips to keep a squeal of excitement from escaping—but she couldn't help smiling from pure joy.

Her bag was packed and leaned against the wall, out of range of the dirty sand pile. She'd already said a long goodbye to the soldiers she'd trained with, written a note to her older sister (who hated goodbyes), stole some jerky from the kitchen, and got in a power nap before her long journey. Now she had to face the hardest part.

Saying goodbye to Da.

He was working on the wall, as usual. The never-ending wall—erected to keep the ruthless King James' army out.

Instead of stopping what he was doing, Da kept his back to her and kept working—she stepped beside him and started cranking the mortar barrel in a circle, keeping it from drying. The mundane work drained some of her excitement.

Da was never so happy as when his fingers were coated in dirt or sand. She was never so happy as when she was surrounded by a cloud, flying.

Da, better known as King Labrencias, was muscular, black, and tall, with spiky hair and a full, curly beard. He leveled the mortar with his scalpel, scraping it up and down. Up and down. It grated on the rough brick. The dust tickled her nose and she sneezed.

The sun was at its zenith, and not a cloud was in the sky. Even the birds were resting in this heat. She wiped her sweaty forehead with the back of her hand, knowing she'd probably left a streak of fine white dust on her black skin. "The sun is melting my brain."

"That's too bad," Da said. "You'll probably need a brain at the Magic Academy."

She gave a wry grin. "Now all they'll get is brain soup."

A wave of nervousness washed over her at the thought of meeting the students from Dram. She only knew a few people who weren't Zoton. What if she made a fool of herself? What if her customs were strange to them?

Pushing back those thoughts, she tried to focus on what really mattered: learning magic. She'd put up with anything to do that.

Though she was powerful, she was inexperienced. She felt like she was in a loop, practicing the same abilities over and over again. But she knew there were so many more out there. She couldn't wait to meet Mage Bahir and learn from him.

Da paused and eyed the brick, making sure it lined up perfectly with the plumb line.

Lace kept the mortar rotating. Her biceps burned from the constant exertion. "I'm going to have arms as stout as a crocodile's tail before the wall's done."

"Is that a bad thing?" Da asked. "Crocs are skilled hunters."

"I'd rather attract a man than a crocodile," Lace said dryly.

He laughed. "You'll just have to find a man who loves you, croc arms and all."

The wind tickled her neck, ruffling the little curls.

Da reached behind him without looking, and Lace put a brick on his hand. "Life is going to be hard at the Magic

Academy," he said as he lowered the brick precisely in its spot.

She gave him another. "Things are hard here too, Da. What with all the training and schoolwork. And don't get me started on the mending . . ."

He wiped his brow. "That's the truth. But we all do our own so it's fair. You just have to do more since you get into so many scrapes." He winked. Sweat dropped from his chin.

A breeze gusted through, a gift from the mountains. Her sister had cut her hair that morning so it was off her neck. She closed her eyes and enjoyed the kiss of the cool wind on her cheeks.

When she opened her eyes, Da was giving her an unfathomable look.

He put his scalpel down and gently laid his hands on her shoulders. She looked up to him, as she always had, and not just because he was taller than her.

"It's a great honor that you've been chosen, yet . . . I wish you didn't have to go," he said in a husky voice. "I wish your mother and grandmother were still alive to teach you the arcane. But the invasion is coming . . ."

She knew. The coming war was a noose around their necks, a cloud over their heads, giving urgency to all their tasks. Lace felt heartsick at every sight of flames in the distance, at every horrified refugee who crossed the border, at every tale of the army who had no mercy.

She put her hands over his, and her throat tightened. "I know, Da. I'll learn from Arch Mage Bahir and be right back. You won't even notice I'm gone."

His eyes were sad. He kissed her on the forehead, then wrapped his arms around her in a great bear hug. She hadn't received one of those since she was a little girl, and her heart swelled to bursting.

"I love you," she mouthed, too quiet for him to hear. Those were words she'd never heard from his mouth. But she knew in the pit of her soul that he loved her.

Da cleared his throat and pulled away. "Always remember that it was a magician that killed your mother." He narrowed his eyes. "You can't trust them. The whole lot of them. Most have been turned into King James' servants. Zoto is for Zoto. No matter what you see out there or who you meet, our country's safety is your priority."

She nodded. "Zoto for Zoto." She looked at the horizon, ready to start this adventure before it became too painful to leave Da. "I'd better fly now so I can reach Moth Valley before sun fall."

"Aye! But first you have to promise me something."

She hefted her leather backpack onto her shoulders and

tied the hip straps. "What is it?"

He secured each pack strap, pulling it tight. "You've got a soft heart and a gentle spirit. You give love too easily—"

Her face got hot. She opened her mouth to protest, but he raised his voice.

"You're much tougher than you used to be. Our country is small and our power tenuous—you must stay faithful to our people. Never put anything before Zoto, you hear?" He offered his arm. "Nothing."

"That is an easy promise to keep." Lace gripped his forearm. "Zoto will always come first."

Chapter Two

Valley of the Moth

Lace soared through the air. The wind pressed back her hair and snapped her skirt against her ankles.

This was a deep cloud—so dense she couldn't see the end of it. It smelled fresh and pure. Water droplets stung her eyes and soaked her clothes. A not-yet-rain bath. She closed her eyes and threaded her aura with the air, pulling it to her. She surged forward in a burst of speed.

Once at the Magic Academy, her world would get so much bigger. She might have a chance at becoming a powerful mage, like her mother. It was her mother who had taught her to fly, passing on the rare magic of melding aura and air. The royal Centurions of King James' army were the only other mages in the world who could do it.

Controlling the air's aura was not her only gift—she

could also see the spirit-bright aura of souls, animals, and magical items. It was something she was born with.

No one had ever been able to lie to her about who they were.

The mist cooled her hot skin. Her shoulders ached from the strain of the flight and weight of her pack. She'd never flown this far before. After six hours in the air, her magic was sorely depleted.

Finally, she soared out of the cloud and caught her breath.

There it was. Valley of the Moth.

It was centered between Zoto's border and Mount Grimstone, the biggest peak in Dram, King James' country. The location was remote. The border was unprotected by soldiers—because Grimstone was nearly impossible to cross.

A river of crystal cool mountain water rushed down a waterfall. Glistening over the pool was a wide rainbow. River otters splashed in the shaded water.

Ancient oak and birch trees, some as wide as the cottages back home, dotted the rocky terrain. The mountain range leveled off into a plain, bursting with wildflowers and lush grass. Butterflies wafted through the green.

Wind gusted across the grass and made it rise and fall like waves of the sea. Even from this height, she smelled fauna and freshwater, two of her favorite scents.

Ah yes, this would do quite nicely for a pseudo-home while she was away from Zoto.

She scanned the valley for auras. However, the place was empty save for birds and a herd of grazing gazelles.

Was she at the wrong location? Spreading her arms, she slowed to a stop and hovered, searching the terrain. But still, no humans.

Sweat dripped off her chin and soaked the edges of her sleeveless dress. Her magic only lasted so long—it weakened just like muscles did. Her powers felt as worn as if she'd just ran the Zoto Mountain Race.

She had an athletic build and great endurance from hours of training with Da's soldiers every day, but this was too much. Even though flying didn't require much power, she'd been in the air for six hours and barely had the strength left to hover.

She shouldered off her leather pack, balancing in the air as best she could, and dug in one of the pockets for the letter. Opening it, she read it for the twelfth time, wondering if she'd missed something:

To His Highness, the Most Excellent Leader of Zoto, King Katel Labrencias the Fourth,

From your most humble servant, the exiled royal Wizard

of Dram, Bahir Tavvakoli,

Whoever treads the path of divine guidance, on him be peace.

I will train seven carefully selected students in arcane lifestyle and skills. I am pleased to inform you that your youngest daughter has been chosen for this Magic Academy.

However, I must be forthright. The purpose of this training is to bring down King James and end his reign of terror. As a border country to Dram, I expect you have noticed how the King's presence grows mighty—surely you feel it bearing down on you and your people.

If you feel the need to protect your country from his hand, I request that you send your child immediately to the Valley of the Moth, at the foot of Mount Grimstone. Please send the student alone and unarmed.

I cannot promise that she will be safe. I can promise that I will give her every mental and physical weapon I have to protect her. I assure you, each candidate was carefully chosen and are the best suited for taking down King James and his ruthless Centurions.

Faithfully yours,

Bahir

Lace frowned and slipped the letter into her pocket. She was certainly alone, and except for the hunting knife she carried on her belt, she was unarmed.

They didn't possibly need her to chuck the knife before they revealed themselves, did they? It seemed too much to ask. That knife was like an extension of her hand.

She scanned the perimeter of the valley again. The herd of grazing gazelle suddenly spooked and galloped toward the river. Wait, what was that? She saw a shadow that had been hiding among them.

It was a man.

Every nerve tightened.

Why the hell couldn't she see his aura?

Something in his hand glowed bright orange with arcane power. What the—?

An arrow whistled by her neck. She jerked away. It was faster than anything she'd ever seen shot from a bow. Then another flashed by, grazing her shoulder. Pain burst and blood trickled down her arm.

She was under attack!

Ducking, she swerved sideways, then lowered altitude. The arrows were impossible—had to be magical. She was out of range of any archer, even the strongest.

Blood seeped through her dress. Her heart hammered in her ears. In the sky she was an easy target. She either had to lose herself in the clouds or charge him.

She grit her teeth.

Lace was never one for running away.

Releasing the aura around her, she dove headfirst. Pointing her toes, she kept her back straight and dropped like a rock from the heights. Free fall. The wind whistled in her ears. The pain in her arm dulled. She felt nothing but the speed, the thrill of her heart, the focus on the fight ahead.

She had to reach the archer before he attacked again.

The ground approached. Lace spread her arms wide and caught the air aura again, swooping into a glide. The grass rushed past in a blur. She sped across the meadow.

Almost there.

His figure became clear. It was a young man, dark and tall, wearing monk's garb. No weapons that she could see. He backed up, lowering, taking a defensive stance.

Lace's face flushed in anger and adrenaline. Her senses felt hot and raw. He kept backing up but she was too fast. Barely slowing down, she plowed him over, her knee in his chest. His heels flew over his head, and he hit the ground with a satisfying *thump.*

She drew her knife, while he skidded on the ground, tearing up grass and flowers.

The battle rage settled over her like a blanket, that unique anger of being in mortal danger—the sharp terror of knowing that a mistake might be her last.

Lace pulled herself to an abrupt stop. The fall had knocked his breath out. He choked and arched his back.

She released the air's aura and landed right on his chest. Her equilibrium was off and for a moment everything swam. Breathing through her nose, she blinked quickly until the world steadied.

He took a gasping breath.

She straddled his broad chest and trapped his arms to his sides with her muscular thighs. He jerked and tried to buck her off. Then she pressed her long blade to his neck. He froze, eyes wide, neck muscles taut.

She felt blind because she was unable to see his aura. What was happening? There must be some counter magic—perhaps his arcane ability—that hid his aura from her. It freaked her out. There had never been a time she hadn't seen someone's soul.

The wind blew her hair back. Her eyes flashed as she sized him up.

Gods, he was handsome.

Too bad she'd probably have to kill him.

His skin was dark, and his hair was brown and disheveled from their fight. His body was muscular and lithe, frozen beneath her. Eyes were the color of sunlight on grass, jaw was set and strong. His smooth cheeks were ageless—was he sixteen or twenty-six? He wore monk's garb: a rough loose tunic over coarse pants. She couldn't tell what sect he was.

Those eyes.

She was taken aback by his intense gaze. His expression was so full of wonder and longing it made her heart quicken. It was as if he was totally unaware of the very dangerous knife at his throat.

"You!" he said.

She blinked, not moving the blade an inch. Then the flicker of a memory rose, a dreadful day, a vision of his terror-stricken face trapped behind fire and death.

Chapter Three
The Animal

Her first day of battle—the week after her joyous coming-of-age ceremony—was the worst day of her life.

She was twelve.

She'd been devoted to the sword and bow since the age of nine, and Mama had trained her in the magical arts every day.

It was time to test her mettle.

Her mother chose a simple mission—there was a band of Pickas Robbers marauding a small seaport. The second time they attacked, they killed two men.

"This is what the royalty are for," Mama said. "To protect our people from greedy men like these."

They went into the Dire Caves, the thieves' hideout. The air smelled of black magic and blood coal. The darkness was like an evil spirit.

They underestimated their enemy. Pickas set a rock trap, released demons on their heads, and had a mage that could control fire. Their fellow soldiers had been decimated after the first round of attacks, but Mama was made of sterner stuff.

She told Lace to run, but Lace stayed at her side, longing to be just as brave as Mama.

Mama went wild, hurling magic and metal, and raining curses on their foes. No one could stand against her. All fell in one manner or the other. Lace had not thought she could love Mama more than she did, but that day her love turned into a fire and etched scars in her heart.

They thought all their enemies were dead. Mama's laugh echoed over the cave walls and she hugged Lace, a last hug, before they went into the thieves' quarters and found the slave. Mama freed him, a boy whose grime and wounds were not enough to hide the unique quality of his aura and the beauty in his eyes.

Those same eyes looked on her now, but they were no longer the frightened eyes of a slave-boy. He was a mage monk, which meant he was powerful and disciplined enough to be accepted into a temple. With a shiver of uncertainty, Lace wondered what he was capable of?

He must be one of those mages who could steal magic—for how else could she not see his aura?

She leaned over the man and gripped the knife tighter. Blood trickled from where her knife met his neck and soaked into his collar.

"Why were you shooting at me?" Her voice was hoarse with adrenaline.

Sweat glistened on his face. He parted his lips as if to speak, then shut them. If she'd been with her father, she'd have killed this man already.

But something in his eyes stayed her hand, and she didn't have her father to command her to do it. He looked completely at a loss, as if the sight of her had stopped his world.

Or maybe that was just her knife.

He was much bigger than her, stronger in every way. He was holding back—and his unreadable aura made him a complete mystery. Her heart raced.

Should she kill him before he killed her?

No . . . not yet.

"Why did you shoot me?" she said again, so close to his face she could smell him. Gritting her teeth, she pressed the knife in.

"King James' Centurions." His accent was lilting and

thick; she couldn't place it. Definitely not from Dram or Zoto. His pulsing heartbeat stayed true, he was not trying to deceive her.

"Aye, what of them?"

"I thought you were one of them. No other mage can fly." His voice made it sound like more of a question than a statement. He flexed his arm as if to throw her off. She squeezed the knife tighter to his throat.

"Do I look like a Centurion?"

He looked her up and down, taking in her dress, jewelry, and dark skin. She leaned back but didn't relinquish any pressure on the knife. He looked at her face, roaming it. No fear at all, only a strange mixture of surprise and something she could not decipher.

Her face flushed at his scrutiny. Looking at him woke something in her. Almost impossible to describe. She'd been with plenty of handsome men, and enjoyed her fair share of pleasures with them—but he was something new. There was a fluid beauty in his features that made her want to stare forever, and something in his eyes that connected—as if he'd been missing from her. She felt a natural primal attraction that scared her more than his arrows did.

"You're-you're—" he stuttered. "Do you remember me?"

"How could I forget?" Her breathing slowed and she became aware of her position over him. She felt the heat of his body and his heartbeat thudding on her inner thigh.

His eyes softened, and his voice was more in control when he spoke again.

"Obviously you're no centurion. Their ugly faces match their ugly souls." He swallowed. "I mean you no harm. Release the knife."

"How can I trust you? The last time we met was the worst day of my life, and here you are shooting arrows at me, thwarting my magic—"

He glanced sharply at her, piercing green. "Thwarting? No. I swear by everything in me that I would die rather than hurt you. I owe you and your mother my life, and I will give it to you in service any chance I get."

He spoke with such familiarity, but she hadn't thought of him once since that day. She stiffened, knowing she could not trust him until his aura was revealed. "Show me your aura or I can never trust you."

The sun shone off the rustling grass. He squinted against the light. "I am not—"

"Shh!" she interrupted.

A red aura appeared out of the corner of her eye, approaching quickly. She looked up, straining to examine the aura.

It was an animal. An old one. Something big.

"What is it?" The man followed her gaze. Blind to the aura, he couldn't see or hear anything.

She felt a steady shake in the ground, a rhythmic vibration. Hooves. Wild animals in this area were just as dangerous as humans, she had to be careful. It galloped right at her back, and there was something strange and heavy about the sound.

"Who's your friend?" she asked coldly.

His eyes widened and the sun reflected off of them. "What? No! I'm not expecting anyone except—" He cut himself off.

"Except who?" She leaned forward. "Tell me now or you'll be sliced thin as sea weed."

His expression hardened. "I'm supposed to meet a magician here. And judging from your pack, I assume you are as well. Except you weren't supposed to bring any weapons."

Her lips parted in surprise.

Was it true? They were both students? Her heart skipped a beat at the thought of sharing a classroom with him. Dammit, if only she could read his aura—then she'd know whether he was lying or not.

She had to test him. “I received the same letter as well. From Drak the Magician.”

At the name, a micro-expression of disgust washed over his face. “No. From his brother, Bahir.”

The animal was now very close. She flicked a glance at the grass but still couldn’t see what it was. She had to take a better position.

“Prove that you’ve been invited.”

“I’ll get the letter.”

His hands flared orange before she could react, and a folded letter identical to hers appeared in the grass. The broken seal had the same insignia she’d received. She felt in her pocket, but her letter was still there. Which meant he’d summoned it, or transfigured it somehow.

The letter proved it. It was marked just like hers—with a flame surrounded by a wreath, Bahir’s seal. He was a student at the magic academy. She bit the side of her lip. Nothing like making a good first impression with a fellow student.

The animal was almost on them.

Lace swung her leg around so she was behind the man. She gripped his chest and kept the knife pressed against his pulsing jugular. Now when the animal came it’d have to get through her body shield first.

A magnificent elk burst through the tall grass.

It had a velvety brown coat with white ears and a star on his forehead. Its haunches and knees had greyed, and his eyes were speckled. This was no young buck. It was also loaded with a powerful yet neutral magical item, and a brand on its chest had Bahir's insignia.

The elk approached at a trot and then stopped in front of them. It snorted and pawed the grass. A gust of wind blew across the meadow.

The monk's hands flared orange once again.

Lace whispered in the man's ear, "I can see if you are about to use magic. Don't even try or I'll gut you."

Then she released him and stood up, sheathing her knife and straightening her skirt.

The monk got to his feet and brushed his pants off. Her eyes edged up his back and wide shoulders, each of his muscles visible through his thin tunic. That was when she noticed the scars on his forearms and neck. Burn marks and knife wounds lined the tender flesh. Gods, this man had been tortured. Before he caught her looking at him, she looked away.

Without meaning to, her heart softened in sympathy for him. Whatever his past was, it wasn't pretty.

The man took a steadying breath, then squared his

shoulders. He held out his hand to her. "You must be Princess Lace of Zoto. It's a pleasure to meet you—under better circumstances this time."

Lace hesitated, then grasped his hand and squeezed—his hand was cool, and so big that hers was nearly lost in it. "Who are you?"

"I am Raj." He paused. "Just Raj."

A simple name for such a complex man. It was like being flipped upside down now that she couldn't read his spirit. She'd have to rely on her words and intuition.

"Where do you come from?" she asked.

He didn't look her in the eye, he scanned the horizon. "From the north."

She set her jaw. Hardness crept back into her heart. That was no answer. He seemed to know more about her than she did about him, and that had never happened to her. It felt awful.

She wanted to ask so many things—what sect of monk he was, how he seemed so familiar with Zoto and the centurions, what he'd done since Mama had saved him from slavery—but she held her tongue. Her tongue always got her into dire straits, and she was deep enough as it was.

The elk stopped in front of them.

Turning to it, Raj said, "What have we got here?"

"It's some kind of message from Bahir. It has a potent magical item on it." She instantly regretted her words. Now he knew her ability. Why did her tongue get so loose when she was nervous?

But he didn't even blink, as if he already knew her ability.

A scent of freshwater and berries reached Lace, making her mouth water. She was parched. A full canteen was too heavy to fly with, and her muscles felt shriveled from lack of water.

And she was starving. Where was Bahir? Maybe this elk would lead them towards some food. They were surrounded by bright orange poppies, waving in the wind. She plucked a flower and absently twirled the stem between her fingers.

The elk stared at them with a dour expression.

"You have a message for us, elk?" she asked.

It snuffed, then brayed.

"I'm sorry. I don't speak your language." She crossed her arms.

It stamped its hoof, snorted, and then leaned its head down and started ripping tufts of grass. Loud chewing filled the air.

They stood in a triangle, girl, boy, elk. Tense and not knowing what to expect.

"You're bleeding," Raj said.

Lace pressed a finger to her cut. It stung, but wasn't deep. "Barely. Good thing you're a bad shot or Bahir would have to find a replacement student."

"I didn't have to miss." His tone was steady—not bragging, but not one to be trifled with either. A flicker of a smile passed his face. "Good thing you're not a bloodthirsty warrior or else Bahir would have to find a replacement for me."

Raj took a step closer, eyeing her shallow wound. "Would you like a bandage?"

"Can you make one appear out of nowhere like you did the arrow?"

He made a rectangle with his fingers and a stark white bandage appeared, fluttering in the breeze. "Nothing comes out of nowhere."

Lace raised her eyebrows. "So you summon it. You know summoning is just a fancy word for stealing? Perhaps that's where all my left stockings have gone, or the box of figs that Da berated me for losing."

He chuckled. "Your stockings aren't my style, but I do have a penchant for figs." He ran the cloth through his fingers. "I got this from King James' stores."

"Well, then . . ." She knew the dangers of infection. Lace

held out her arm and he wrapped the soft fabric carefully around the wound. Each layer lined up with the last, orderly and neat. His breath was shallow as he leaned over her. He'd either performed this task a hundred times or he was good with his hands. Her heart beat faster, and a dot of red appeared on the white.

As soon as he tucked the wrapping in, the wound felt better. The constant pressure relieved the throbbing.

The scrape on his neck had already scabbed over, or else she'd offer to bind it. Or perhaps he'd never want her near his neck again.

The elk suddenly drew near.

"Ah, you've come to join us," Raj said, reaching for its velvety nose.

Lace felt the magical aura change. It was vibrating, getting bigger, deepening and swirling. It aimed like a great spear at them.

"Get back!" Lace screamed, pulling Raj away from it.

A string of light lassoed Lace's shoulders. All the breath was pulled from her lungs. She felt like she was yanked out of her body.

Then everything went black.

Chapter Four
The Little Girl

Lace awoke with a gasp. Her chest heaved. It hurt like hell, as if her lungs were being twisted. Someone screamed in her ear, soul-wrenching and horrified, but it sounded muffled. Oh gods, what was happening?

She couldn't open her eyes or move in the slightest. Her body was frozen. Trapped in a spell. A cold sweat covered her, her eyes burned, and her breath caught in her throat.

Was this how she would die? Trapped in a paralytic spell was one of the worst ways to go.

The screaming stopped, and muffled voices took its place.

Think, Lace, think.

Panic clouded every thought, twisting and ripping until her mind felt both empty and full at the same time.

First she needed to be calm. Then she needed to think. Deep breath in. Deep breath out. In. Out. Slowly, she gained a semblance of control.

How could she break this spell?

A female voice came closer—vibrations shook her back, as if a herd of people were approaching. But auras weren't appearing. This had never happened before. For as long as she could remember she'd always felt auras approach, even when her eyes were closed. Where had her magic gone? Was this all Raj's fault?

Another scream resounded in Lace's face, so loud it made her ears ring.

She still couldn't feel anything.

A little voice broke into sobs. The cries were heartbreaking. It sounded like a child, and Lace melted in pity. What was happening to her?

Suddenly Lace felt as if wind gusted through her blood stream. Pain burned through her, she gave a low groan. Her skin tingled and pricked as if tiny needles pressed into her.

Then her body unlocked. Muscles revived. Energy flooded through her. The spell was broken!

She opened her eyes and sat up abruptly, panting. The meadow was gone. She was surrounded by stone walls. Holy hell. That wasn't just a spell, she'd been transported!

Lace's chest burned from lack of oxygen. Her vision swam and heart pounded. Gods, the spell had a harsh aftertaste. Whoever cast it was not scadding around.

Now was the time to run. Fast.

She reached for the air's aura to lift her, but nothing happened. With a grunt, she spread her fingers and cast her magic. But there was none. Her being was cold and empty—the warm glow of magic that always accompanied her was gone. For a moment, it felt like her heart was ripped from her. Panic rose, clouding her thoughts. Without magic, she was powerless!

How could she get out of here without it?

Her skirt was tangled around her legs and the strap had slipped off her shoulders. She gave a sharp glance at her surroundings. Where was she? Her senses charged, she was wide-eyed, expecting an attack.

Two towering walls surrounded her, at least twice her height. It was a stone hallway—narrow and ancient—covered with pungent vines.

Layers of greenery covered the rough hewn stones. It smelled of fresh dirt and rotting leaves, old and stagnant. No wind or sun smiled on her. The clouds were thick and stormy-gray, so low it felt like a ceiling was closing in on her.

Raj lay unconscious beside her, face down on the

walkway. She leaned over him and pressed two fingers against his neck. A steady rhythm beat. His face pressed against the stone so she gently lifted his head onto her lap and brushed his long, coarse hair out of his face.

Suddenly, adrenaline coursed through her. She had the feeling of being watched, of being in danger.

This was a trap.

Scad. They weren't alone!

Hunched over and rocking on her heels, a girl had her back to Lace. Her face was shielded by a shawl.

A shiver of dread washed over Lace.

Even without her magic she had a bad feeling about this girl. But how could she know? She couldn't judge the girl's aura, and it was obvious the child was in distress.

Raj groaned and pushed himself up, sitting cross legged. He put his head in his hands, wincing at the pain of the curse. "Oh no, no, no!" His green eyes suddenly flew open, and for a second she saw the open terror she'd seen in his face as a boy. "My magic is gone!" He looked young and vulnerable, which turned Lace's heart. She set a hand on his shoulder.

"I'm here," she whispered.

He placed his hand over hers, then kissed his other hand and held it to the sky in a prayer of thanks. "Thank the gods." His grip on her was urgent, as if he let go he'd be lost.

They sat in silence for a moment. At his touch and presence, her mind cleared and the adrenaline drained. For a moment, all she felt was the connection with Raj, his warm skin, his even breathing. It steadied her.

"I need my magic back," he said.

She nodded, silently.

Wait, what was she doing? She couldn't even see his aura! He could be lying—could be the one stealing power from her. Slipping her hand out of his, she rubbed her sore arm, clenching and unclenching her fists to keep the blood pumping. What was it about him that made her put her guard down?

Though the sun was hidden, it was humid enough to coat her in a light sheen of sweat.

He groaned again, then stood, offering his hand to help her up. "You know what this has taught me?"

She ignored his hand and stood. "Never trust an elk?"

"No."

"That Bahir was compromised, or he sent the letter to trap us?"

He gave a wan smile. "No. I learned it feels damn awful to be on the receiving end of the Paralytic Curse." He rubbed his temples. "I feel like I've been crushed between a hippo's teeth."

She felt a jolt of apprehension knowing that he could do the curse. That was magic beyond her. What other powers did he have?

"Where are we?" He looked around, then froze when he saw the little girl.

She hadn't moved. She stayed in the shadows, back turned, shivering.

Whatever trepidation Lace felt at the sight of her, Raj felt none. He hurried towards her.

"Wait," Lace said, reaching for him.

He turned, questioning.

"She-she-she is—" Lace stuttered, not sure how to phrase her instinct. "Be careful." Some people believed magic was simply heightened instincts. If that was true, she had to trust her gut.

"What? Why?" He walked backwards towards the girl, locking eyes with Lace, yet anxious to help.

How could she explain the impressions she had? It'd be like trying to describe a jellyfish to someone who had never seen one. "I don't know," Lace finally said, feeling silly. She felt that the girl was dangerous. But she was so tiny and helpless, how could that be? If she could see the girl's aura, Lace would know in one second. Her face grew warm, embarrassed and frustrated at the loss of her gifts.

Who was she without them?

Raj reached the girl and knelt in front of her. The crying lessened. Lace followed, the damp soil clinging to her sandals. The floor was spongy with dirt and moss covering the stone.

She stood behind him, unconsciously setting her hand on the handle of her knife.

The little girl took a shuddering breath, then looked up at them. She had to be no more than seven years old. Her silky black hair hung down like a curtain over half her face. Her beautiful pure skin brought out sharp black eyes, big and framed with long lashes. She glanced over Raj, then stared up at Lace.

The longer she looked into the girl's eyes, the more convinced she became that this was no mewling child. Hints of soul peeked out, old and cunning.

"Are you hurt?" He made a soothing sound and gently touched her shoulder.

Raj obviously didn't see any hint of the maturity that Lace saw.

The little girl shook her head so hard her hair waved. She hiccupped and wiped her eyes. Lace glanced around, hyper aware of her surroundings. There was no way she'd be surprised again.

Lace folded her arms across her chest and backed toward the wall, careful not to touch the leaves. They had a sheen to them, which promised some kind of sap or poison.

"Are you alone?" Raj asked.

The little girl nodded.

"What's your name?" he asked.

She stared off into space, slowly blinking.

Lace and Raj exchanged a worried look.

After a long moment, she said, "Kaina." She swallowed. "I'm Kaina. And my Uncle Bahir was supposed to meet me at his house, but before I could get there I was transported here. It hurt! And-and-and I don't know where I am." Her voice quivered and cracked, and Lace was afraid she might start bawling again.

"Well, I'm Raj. I'll take care of you until we find our way back to Uncle Bahir."

She straightened and held out her hand. "You promise?" Lace thought there was a hint of manipulation behind her voice.

Raj nodded and took it. "Promise."

Lace would promise no such thing. Not until she knew for sure Kaina was exactly who she said she was. "So, Kaina." Lace tried to keep her voice gentle. "Where does your Uncle Bahir live?"

"In Moth Valley," the child said.

That couldn't be! Lace gave her a skeptical look. "We just came from Moth Valley. Nothing there except an elk."

Kaina and Raj stood and she took a step toward him, hiding in the crook of his arm. "He doesn't live on the valley, he lives under it." Her eyes widened and tears threatened to spill. "I hope King James hasn't captured him." She looked around. "I hope King James hasn't captured us!"

Fear sliced through her at the thought. If King James stopped the Magic Academy before it began, then he'd stopped the greatest threat against him. Lace felt the weight of needing to protect Zoto wash over her. "Yeah, but why wouldn't King James just kill us? He could have used something stronger than a paralytic curse," Lace said. "Are you sure this isn't your uncle, trying to—"

"My uncle would never do something like this." Kaina wiped her nose with the back of her hand. "I'm hungry."

"Me too." Lace sighed. When Lace could see auras she knew exactly when someone lied—their aura split. But now she had no idea, not even a gut feeling about whether Kaina was telling the truth. Maybe if she could get a handle on some baseline answers then she'd be able to tell when there was a lie. "How old are you?"

Kaina's mouth twitched. "I'm seven."

She studied the round face and still, black eyes. Damn. The only thing Lace felt certain of was that she couldn't tell if Kaina was lying.

"How old are you?" Kaina looked up at Raj.

"Twenty-two," he answered.

She didn't mean to be rude, but she had to try to see more behind Kaina. There was something off about her and she couldn't place it. "What's your magic ability?"

The little girl hid her face in the back of Raj's shirt. He gave a little laugh and twisted to try and see her, but she just shadowed him. "I don't think she's ready for questions," he said.

Or she was just avoiding them.

They started walking down the immense hallway. There was nowhere else to go, and they needed to find the way out.

Lace led, her steps tentative. She glanced over her shoulder to see Raj tense and defensive, ready for anything.

Without her magic she'd have to wholly rely on her skills with the blade.

Kaina looked on the verge of having another meltdown. "I'm really, really hungry!"

Raj leaned in front of her, eyebrows raised. "Sometimes when I'm hungry I imagine what I'm going to eat next. Want to do that?"

Her eyes brightened. "Eel soup!"

Raj laughed. "You like that? Most children don't."

Lace didn't think Kaina was like "most children."

"And fried bread," she went on, "and seaweed rolls, and tomato salad, and chocolate torte for dessert."

"Why not have two deserts?" Lace said. "And eat them first?

"No way," Raj said. "You'll ruin her pretend supper."

Kaina's eyes sparkled, and Lace shot a quick appreciative glance at Raj. At least the girl wasn't crying anymore. "I *will* have two," Kaina said. "Chocolate torte and apple cream pie."

Lace's stomach growled.

"What will you have?" Kaina asked.

"My very favorite in all the world," Raj said with a completely straight face, "First, cow eyeballs. Then, fried cockroaches, roasted duck brains, and bean curd." Kaina giggled. "And for desert I'll have jellied cow nose. Care to join me, Princess?"

She shook her head with a grin but quickly wiped the mirth off her face. "Stay focused on threats, stay alive," Da had always said. Keeping her gaze straight forward, she concentrated on their surroundings.

"Aren't monks supposed to survive on the dew from

heaven? And rice?" Kaina asked.

Raj's voice quieted. "I'm no monk. Not anymore."

That was odd. Most sects believed in eternal devotion. "You're a monk in disguise?"

"I don't have any money for new clothes," he said.

"What're you having for supper, Lace?" Kaina said, skipping a little.

Gods.

Lace had not told Kaina her name. How did she know it? Had Raj whispered it to her when Lace couldn't hear? Danger seemed all around. Lace's eyes trailed from the top of the wall down to the walkway, to the top of the other side, then back again and again, watching for shadows or movement.

"I'll have a let's-not-die-in-a-mysterious-maze with a side of figure-out-who-captured-us, and get-the-hell-back-home for dessert," Lace said.

Raj made a clicking noise. "You have strange dishes in Zoto."

She was suddenly so tired she felt shaky. The adrenaline had worn off and now she was just worn out.

Lace walked down the hallway, her footsteps silent. The end could either be closed or . . . she reached it and saw another walkway to the right, long and enclosed. Identical to the one they were in. Her heart sank.

They were in a maze.

Good things *never* happened to people stuck in a maze. She felt even more powerless than she had before.

"Any idea where we are?" Raj said.

Lace straightened her shoulders. "I'm not as worried about where as *why*. Now that someone brought us here, what will they do to us?

Chapter Five

Never Trust a Pirate

If only Lace could fly for even a minute, she could gain perspective and see a way out of the maze. Each step down the hallway filled her with more dread. They were someone's pawns and had no control.

She had to take back control.

They reached the end of another hallway. Lace gripped her knife and turned the corner.

A rustle of clothes—someone grabbed her arm and jerked her off balance.

She stumbled into a hard chest, iron-like arms locking around her. The man backed up swiftly, holding her. Her breath hitched. Gritting her teeth, she shoved her knife up. The man dodged and her knife caught air. He grabbed her wrist, crushing and twisting her arm until she felt like the bones would break.

Lace dropped her knife.

He draped his arm across her shoulder and trapped her against him, covering her mouth.

The cold tip of a knife pressed against her throat. And a whisper in her ear, "Don't move, luv, or you'll be cut into shark bait."

It'd happened so fast Raj hadn't even turned the corner yet.

She went completely still, hoping he'd loosen his hold so she could attack again. But if anything, he held her closer. And he was so tall that her feet didn't touch the ground. Her hair pressed into his neck. She smelled a waft of the docks: fish and salty air.

Raj turned the corner and froze. His face conveyed no emotion when he saw her. Kaina screamed and collapsed in fear, hiding behind Raj.

"Drop your knife, monk," the man said. "Or this pretty one dies. You have enough blood on your hands already."

Wait, did they know each other?

Raj slowly held his knife in front of him, bending his knees, shoulders taut, as if to drop the weapon. Then he flashed Lace a glance. Somehow she knew exactly what it meant.

Move.

With a knife at her throat, there was only one direction to go. She snapped her neck back, smashing the man in the jaw. He grunted in pain. She twisted her hips and he turned, trying to keep hold of her.

Raj threw his knife.

It flew straight for the man's shoulder. His reflexes were sharp though and he jumped, dodging the weapon. But the distraction was enough to lessen his hold on her.

She grabbed his wrist and pushed, almost wrenching free of his grasp.

Turning, she hit him with a stunning blow in the sensitive nerve between the neck and shoulder. He dropped her.

She ducked and grabbed her knife from the ground. He still hadn't recovered, and she kneed him in the stomach. He doubled over with a grunt. It was all done without a thought. Once she had the use of her arms, unarming a man was as natural to her as breathing.

Taking a step back, she swung the knife through the air. The young man backed up quickly, holding his ribs and limping from the blow. His features were striking—he had clean dark hair, a neatly trimmed beard, and tan skin with tiny wrinkles that indicated he was out in the weather a lot.

Colorful tattoos covered his arms and hands. His clothes were well tailored. No doubt his black leather boots cost more than her family's food for a month. He eyed her with distaste.

She kept her knife steady and tried to keep her voice from shaking. "Back off!" she said through panting breaths. Raj came quickly to her side, and she felt her position much more defensible with him there. Her heartbeat evened.

The men exchanged a glance, staring hard at each other.

The stranger moved back a few steps. Now that she could get a proper look at him, there was something familiar about his face, but she couldn't place him. Damn, if only she could see his aura!

He had a golden necklace on, and a silver eyepiece hanging around his neck—she'd bet a month of chores that it was magical. Two sabers hung at a belt on his waist and an ornate knife was attached to a leather belt crossing his chest.

"Why'd you try to kill me?" Lace said.

He cocked his chin. "If I wanted to kill you, you'd be dead."

Raj's voice was rough. "Bastard."

The man clicked his tongue. "Monks shouldn't say such naughty words."

"Monks are known to be good judges of character," Lace

said, stepping closer to Raj.

The man glared at Raj. "I tell you the truth, sweetheart, if you like good characters then you'll stay far away from that man. Even criminals consider him vile."

Nothing in her said to trust the pirate over the monk. But she couldn't lie to herself—despite the attraction she felt, she really knew nothing about Raj.

Tentative, she took a step away from Raj.

"Lace," Raj said. "Don't listen to him. There-there are things about that story that nobody knows—" he shot the man a hard glance. "He's taking King James' side of the tale. Don't think me vile."

She couldn't read his expression, though something in her wove into his words—connecting and understanding. Was that her natural instinct? Or was she simply melting at the words of a handsome man?

"There are *always* two sides," Lace said. "And we always believe we're in the right. That's part of our nature." From the corner of her eye, Lace saw Kaina stand. "Stay back," Lace ordered. Wide eyed, Kaina sat down again.

It smelled like rain and the gray clouds lowered further, making the space feel more claustrophobic than ever.

Lace put her hand on her narrow hip and faced the man. "What's your story?"

"I was alone in this labyrinth, and then suddenly you appear out of nowhere."

"Nothing comes from nowhere," Raj said. "We were pulled from the Valley of the Moth and would like to return."

An almost imperceptible flash of surprise crossed his face.

"Who are you?" Lace asked.

Raj clenched his jaw. "And what the hell are you doing here?"

The young man smirked, inclining his head. "I'm Captain Black Sky. My name speaks for itself."

Lace's face lit in recognition. "I've seen your posters. You've a bounty on your head for more than two-hundred thousand!" Warming at the thought of seeing someone so famous, she almost grinned. "I've never been in a room with one of King James' most wanted criminals."

"Not just one—" Black Sky murmured, looking at Raj.

"Is that the name your mother gave you?" Lace chuckled to hide her unease.

"Who says I have a mother?" He grinned, but there was no light behind it. "Don't you know the kraken and behemoth raised me on squid ink for breakfast and fire fish for dessert?"

Raj gave him a brief glance. "A man who won't speak his

own name is a coward."

He snorted. "*You* speak to *me* of cowardice?"

Lace noticed Black Sky's hands trembled, and she wondered if he wasn't speaking like this out of nervousness rather than bravado. He didn't look older than she was, and she'd just turned nineteen.

He glanced at Lace and stuck his hands in his pockets. "Call me Arif."

"A reef?" she repeated.

"Aye. Arif."

Lace looked him up and down. "You know what I just can't believe?"

"How incredibly handsome I am?" he said with a crooked grin.

She pursed her lips. "Why did Black Sky leave his ship and crew to study magic at school? *On land?*"

He gave a laugh, though it seemed to mask a deep hurt. "I haven't drunk nearly enough gin to answer you. That's a story for another day."

She longed to see his aura—it must be interesting. He was a ferocious pirate, yet he was also rumored to give every coin he stole to the elders of his village. His expensive outfit said otherwise. How much of this man was righteous vigilante and how much was bloodthirsty barbarian?

"Were you transported here?" Raj asked.

Arif nodded.

"Let me guess . . ." Lace took the letter out of her pocket. "You have one of these?"

A shadow crossed his face. He hesitated, then took an identical letter from his pocket.

"Oh, gods, give me strength," Raj whispered and raised his eyes to the sky in supplication.

The clouds spit mist. It coated Lace's hair, and the chill moisture raised goose-bumps on her arm.

A warm presence came up behind Lace, then Kaina put a hand in hers. "You're all a part of this Magic Academy," she said in a small voice.

What a strange collection of mages. Child, monk, pirate, princess. They couldn't get much different than this.

Raj looked around. "I expected a hall and desks and books and maybe some . . . I don't know . . . teachers."

"We're being played," Lace said. "This is no academy. We need to find a way out of here." And she had to do it alone. There was no one she could trust.

"Ah, so we're friends now?" Arif winked at Lace, his brown eyes shining.

"None of my friends pillage and kill peaceful merchants," Raj said bitterly.

"None of my friends put knives at my throat," Lace added.

Arif put his hands in a praying position and bowed low. "I'm deeply regretful for that violent action. I hate troubling such a beautiful girl." He straightened. "I thought you were an enemy."

Lace took a few steps back, holding Kaina's hand. She touched the bandage where Raj had wounded her earlier with his magic arrows. "Seems like both of you have that in common."

Raj looked side-eyed at Arif, who gazed at Lace unperturbed.

"Good thing they failed," Kaina said.

"I just hope the next student won't succeed," Lace said. "I wonder how many more of us there are?"

Suddenly, a scream echoed through the stone hallway.

Chapter Six
The Sand

The soul-searing scream cut through the air. It was a woman's voice in dire need.

Then the voice cut off.

Lace released Kaina's hand and bolted. She hiked her skirt up to her thighs and sprinted down the hallway, hearing the men's footsteps behind her.

She pushed off the ground as fast as she could, shouldering back, taking deep even breaths, kicking off the rough ground. Her long legs ate up the distance. At the end of the hallway she turned right, then ground to a halt.

A woman and man were in the middle of the hallway, up to their shoulders in sinking sand. The beautiful woman's eyes were round and horrified. Her chest heaved as she slipped deeper. The man, who was bigger than anyone Lace had ever seen, was wrestling and twisting, reaching for the wall, straining with all his might for something to hold onto. He only had one eye, scarred white and blind.

"Stop struggling," she called to the man as she raced towards them. "You'll only sink faster."

He eyed her distrustfully but stopped moving. The woman cried out and reached for Lace.

Lace had dealt with quicksand before. There were large sections of it in Zoto which had to be navigated. But she'd never experienced it in a labyrinth full of magic and mystery . . . would it be different here?

It was clear where the quicksand started. Lace stopped just inches before it, right on the edge. The man and woman were up to their shoulders now, slipping fast. Lace caught the woman's bright green eyes.

"Please, help!" she said.

Raj skidded to a halt behind her. "What do we do?" he asked, out of breath.

"Give me your belt," she ordered as she shouldered out of her pack and undid the straps. Raj pulled his belt off and placed it in her hand, it had red beads sewn onto smooth, oiled black leather. He held up his loose linen pants with one hand.

"That's my prayer belt," he said.

"And it's about to answer someone's prayer," Lace said. Kneeling, Lace gripped the belt and threw the other end at the woman. "Grab hold."

The woman strained with all her might, but there was at least a foot difference. Not long enough! Sand slid over her shoulders and she cried out. The man still hadn't said a word. His lips were pursed, and he looked in alarm from Lace to the woman.

They would suffocate unless Lace got them out in the next few seconds.

"Raj, lower me closer," she said, voice laced in panic. Raj grabbed her wrist and she grabbed his, and he gently leaned until she balanced sideways over the sand. If she didn't trust Raj to hold her up, these people would die.

Arif's voice cut in from behind. "Don't risk your life for a stranger. Are you crazy?"

Lace ignored Arif and threw the belt again. The sand was up to the woman's chin, but her hands were raised. That's what Lace aimed for. This time it was far enough but she missed her throw, landing to the left.

The woman's face grew red and she started hyperventilating. Her mouth pulled down in horror.

"Try to stay calm," Lace said as she snapped the belt back. The sand was up to the woman's nose. Her breath cratered the sand. Lace took a deep breath before the throw. This was her last chance.

"You can do it," Raj said, his tone reassuring.

She threw one end of the belt. It hit the girl in the face. The woman gasped, then instantly grabbed it with both hands and yanked, almost pulling the belt out of Lace's grip.

"Now! Steady." She strained with all her might, her muscles bulging. The woman rose. Lace took a big breath and pulled with all her might. The woman's neck appeared, and then her shoulders wriggled out of the sand. She was strong, pulling herself along the belt hand after hand. "Take us up, Raj," Lace said.

"One, two, three," Raj counted, and then all of Lace's joints stretched as he pulled, carrying both of them up. Sand sprayed everywhere as the woman scrambled out of the pit. Raj took their arms and dragged them to safety.

They collapsed on to the rocks, panting.

In a gasping, urgent voice, the woman leaned back towards the pit. "Save One Eye!"

He was covered in sand up to his chin, and sinking fast.

Lace stared at him. Was she strong enough to carry such a big man? His arm was bigger than her leg. Her joints might tear.

But she had to try.

"We need a longer rope. Now!" Lace said.

"I don't have another belt," Raj said. She shot a glance at Arif—who backed up even more. He wasn't sharing his. And there wasn't time to fight him for it.

"Think, think, think," she whispered. She jumped up and grabbed her pack and knife, then sliced off the straps in a fluid motion. She tied the belt to the metal hinges from the backpack straps and yanked them tight.

"Hurry!" the woman said. "He's almost gone!"

One Eye's mouth was covered. He tilted his nose to be able to breath.

Without even asking, Raj took the belt and wrapped it around his knuckles and threw it to One Eye. The extra length brought it close enough.

One Eye lunged and grabbed it, almost yanking Raj off balance. Grunting, Raj strained against the straps, which stopped One Eye from sinking further but wasn't pulling him out.

Lace stood behind Raj and wrapped her arms around his chest, steadying him. "One, two, three," he whispered, then they both leaned back simultaneously.

One Eye rose, but just barely. He took a gasping breath and spit sand out of his mouth.

The woman got to her feet and ran behind Lace,

gripping her shoulders. "One, two, three," Raj said, and they pulled back together.

They barely got him out another inch. It was as if he was made of pure iron.

Just as they were about to pull again, two little arms gripped her, pulling on Lace's waist. She looked back to see Kaina behind the woman, red faced, pulling as hard as she could.

Arif stared from a little ways off, his arms crossed, frowning.

"Let's do it," Lace said. "This is it."

"One. Two. Three," Raj shouted, then pulled, every sinew taut. Lace leaned back, helped by the pull from the woman and Kaina. Just as it seemed like One Eye would never move, his entire torso shot out of the sand.

All of them flew back and landed in a heap.

Raj scrambled to his feet and kept pulling, so as not to lose any momentum. One Eye twisted to stay free of the depths as Raj dragged him to safety.

The burly man stayed on his back, taking deep breaths. The woman ran to him and knelt beside him. She stroked his cheek and brushed the sand from his whiskers.

Lace didn't need to see auras to know they were a couple. Her heart melted at the relieved glances of love they gave each other.

Taking up her torn backpack, she sighed. Now she'd have to carry it by the handle until there was enough time to mend it. She sighed again. More mending. It was full of her supplies and everything in it smelled of home, so there was no way she'd leave it.

She took out a slim knife and slipped it into her belt.

This place was dangerous. She felt someone's eyes on her, then looked up to find Raj watching her. "Your smarts saved them," he said.

The compliment was so unexpected she didn't know what to say.

He took a small step towards her. "And for a minute there, you trusted me." At the soft look in his eye, her heart warmed. It was true. There was something between them that she trusted, though she couldn't explain it.

But after what Arif brought up, that mysterious tie wasn't enough. Breaking his gaze, she brushed the sand from her layered skirt.

"I'll earn your trust, Lace," Raj said in his strange accent. It took an active will to not reach for him and reassure him—but she held back. He took a few steps away, giving her room.

One Eye stood, and she saw just how large he actually was. Easily over six and a half feet, he looked tougher than an old desert dragon. He was covered in scars and burns—either war wounds or torture scars—and wore only thin leather pants and boots. On his neck was King James' brand—he'd been a slave—and King James treated his slaves like he did his cattle, if not worse.

The man had a saber at each hip and a sheathed dagger attached to a belt across his chest. His hair was cut very close to his head. One eye was sea-blue and the other scarred white. Because of his blindness, he cocked his head at a funny angle and jerked it from side to side, so he could see from his left.

The woman was the opposite of him. Sweet-faced, skin as clear and soft as a child's, thin arms, not even a knife at her belt. She had frizzy light brown hair, unkempt, with four or five dried flowers braided in the tresses. Her eyes were deep hunter green, her lips bright pink, her skin glowing, with a few freckles dotting her nose and forehead. She wore a tattered, modest blue dress which had been patched many times. It was hard to guess, but Lace thought she looked to be in her mid-twenties.

As quick as thought, One Eye stepped in front of the girl and drew his saber. Lace's heart jumped.

Chapter Seven
One Eye and Violet

"Scad!" Arif cursed, drawing his saber.

Raj stepped in front of Lace with his hands up His expression was open, with no threat. "Peace." He said. "I want nothing but peace."

Lace backed up, hiding Kaina behind her. Her eyes wide, she tried to guess what kind of threat he saw in them. They'd just saved him!

"Hey, hey, hey," Lace said quickly. "I very much want to be very good friends with you. As I do all tall, strong people."

There was a gleam in the man's one eye, and his face relaxed. Lace kept talking. "You look so strong, like you could kill two stones with one bird. Or cut a knife with butter."

"You look like you could make onions cry," Raj said,

catching on.

"He's one of the king's gladiators." Arif cried out, looking like he'd lunge at the giant any second. One Eye glanced from person to person, accessing the situation. "Everyone knows there's no magic allowed in the pits. Maybe he's the one stealing our magic!"

Lace's brow furrowed.

"We aren't thieves," the woman said from behind him, her voice was light and airy. "Except for a few of my aunt's pies when I was little—and who can refuse berry pie?"

"No one," Lace said firmly. "Everyone here has stolen pies at one time or another, I'll wager."

Raj nodded, eyeing the blade. "Not even the gods were able to bestow upon me enough self control to not steal a pie or two."

"Aye, that's right," the woman said. "We're pie thieves, not magic-thieves—that's like stealing the soul. None of these people look evil, One Eye, please take their peace." She stepped out from the shadow of One Eye with a tentative look. He lowered his saber but didn't sheath it. "So . . . everyone else has lost their magic too?"

Everyone looked from one to the other.

Lace's stomach sunk. If everyone had lost theirs—what if they never got it back?

"This is terrible, terrible, terrible," the woman kept repeating the word as she looked around at the maze, her eyes wide and frightened. "It's not what the mage promised."

The tension in the air was palpable. The walls seemed closer than ever before. Though there still was no sign of the sun, the place grew muggy. Sweat dripped down Lace's forehead and coated her back.

"Let me guess," Arif said to the couple. "You're Magic Academy students?"

One Eye and the woman exchanged a look, then nodded.

Arif turned and stomped down the hallway, slicing with his knife and then sheathing it. "Dammit. Why the hell would Bahir send all his students here?" He pointed at everyone in a sweeping gesture. "One of you bastards are stealing my magic." His voice betrayed his panic.

Raj raised his voice. "Watch your language, Pirate." He motioned with his eyes to Kaina.

Arif kept walking down the hallway, shoulders tense, gait stiff. "I'm not battling this maze weighed down with children and savages on top of having no magic. Stay out of my way, all of you."

As she watched him go, Lace felt an intense premonition that he was not to leave them. It was strong enough to make her heart skip a beat and her breath hitch. If she could see auras, she'd have a better idea of why she had the feeling. But she still couldn't see, so she had to trust herself.

"STOP," Lace commanded.

Arif stopped. But didn't turn.

Lace unsuccessfully tried to release the anger from her voice. "We're meant to do this together," she said. "There could be more coming against us than just sand traps. Things we need to beat together."

It felt like a piece of the machine was missing if he left. "You can't sail a ship alone, Black Sky."

Arif took another step away, then paused. "I do everything alone."

"That's scad!" Lace shouted, then cast a guilty look at Kaina. Arif kept walking. "You've drunk too much salt water if you believe that. No one can sail a ship alone."

He stalked angrily down the long hallway, not listening to her.

Moisture beaded on everything—damp mist fell from the sodden sky. She took a deep breath and turned back to the group. Kaina looked scared, and Lace couldn't read Raj's expression.

"No one's seen Bahir?" the woman asked with a worried frown.

Everyone shook their head.

"Can anyone find my magic?" she asked hopefully.

"Yours is hiding somewhere with mine," Lace said.

Kaina's lip quivered and her face reddened. "Do you think Uncle Bahir is safe?" She tugged on Lace's arm. "Are we all going to die here?"

Lace shook her head, and though the girl acted troubled, she couldn't shake the feeling that she wasn't troubled, that her heart was beating steady despite her tears.

Raj said what she was thinking. "Bahir could be the one behind this."

Kaina gasped and pulled away from Lace. One Eye raised his eyebrows and gave a firm shake of his head.

"Bahir would never do that," the woman said. Her voice was beautiful. Soft and musical, with a bit of a drawl to her accent. "He wouldn't save us just to kill us again."

"What do you mean?" Lace asked.

The woman slipped her hand into One Eye's. "We were captives in the Hexagon. One Eye was a gladiator, trained since he was young. I've been a slave there for two years."

Lace's stomach turned. The Hexagon was an underground fighting and sex-slave ring of King James.' Huge fights and orgies took place there. That explained all of One Eye's scars. At the thought of what they'd been through,

Lace's face flushed in anger. They'd probably experienced more agony than Lace could imagine.

"It was Bahir who rescued us," the woman said. "Just last week. He said he could use our abilities at his academy—" she paused, then added, "We'd do anything for him."

"I imagine you have an angry king on your trail now," Lace said.

The woman nodded. Lace realized she still didn't know her name. She placed her hand over her heart and curtsied. "I'm Lace Labrencias, Crown Princess from Zoto. It's a pleasure to meet you."

That was the moment One Eye sheathed his sword. Perhaps he trusted people from Zoto. Or trusted princesses. Or maybe his arm was getting tired.

With a shy smile, the woman curtsied back. "I'm no princess. Never even seen one until now." She grinned. "I'm Violet. I grew up just south of the toxic jungle." That region was a very poor part of Dram, riddled with disease and slavery. "And this is my friend, One Eye. He doesn't speak that I know of."

It was obvious from the way Violet slipped her hand into One Eye's to the way he looked at her that they were more than friends.

Raj shook One Eye's hand. "I'm Raj. The little one is

Kaina. And the grumpy pirate is Arif. We're all students."

Violet glanced around. "We were supposed to meet Bahir in the Valley of the Moth, but we got caught by a portal and transported here."

Lace looked up, her usual escape being to fly. "We should climb the wall and see what's out there."

Violet looked closer at the thick vines clinging to the walls. Their edges were serrated, and tiny purple flowers blossomed on the stem. "That's poison luke," she said. "Nobody touch it or they'll be—"

"Poisoned?" Lace finished.

Violet nodded. "You'd be dead in less time than it takes to cut off the poisoned flesh. A horrible way to die."

"I don't like this one bit," Lace said, walking up and down in front of the quick sand. "Not very neighborly of whoever brought us here to put sand traps in—"

A loud *snap* came from the long end of the hallway—from the direction Arif had gone.

"Uh-oh," Kaina said.

A rumble of rock on rock. The ground trembled and the leaves shook. Everyone looked back, then froze.

Arif sprinted towards them. The wall behind him was moving. It grated across the floor like a bookend on a shelf, pressing towards them.

The wall kept closing in. And it was gaining speed.

"Run!" Arif shouted. "This wall is trying to kill me!"

Chapter Eight
Trapped

They were trapped. The quicksand was on one side, and it was too far to jump over it—but when she looked across the floor, the sinking sand was gone.

A chill went through her.

One minute they'd saved One Eye and Violet from the sand, and the next minute the sand was gone. As if they'd only imagined it. One minute Arif left the group, and now he was being chased by the wall. Where the hell were they?

No time to figure it out. The wall was coming, and it was coming fast.

"Let's go," Violet said in a calm voice.

Without hesitation, One Eye took Kaina in his arms. He hefted her up as if she were a rag doll, and she put her arm around his neck. He started running for the end of the hall.

Lace grabbed handfuls of her skirt. Lifting it above her knees with one hand and her bag in the other, she sprinted. She looked over her shoulder. The wall sped at them. It snapped and swallowed the vines, crushing them in its path. It moved with a squeaky grating sound, clicking rhythmically as if propelled by a machine.

The pungent smell of crushed poison luke pervaded the hall.

She and Raj had effortless strides and kept pace together. It had been awhile since she'd run for her life—most of the time she flew. She kept reaching for the air's aura, kept pushing off the earth in order to fly. But there was nothing to pull her up.

"Now would be a good time to get my magic," she said in a breathless voice.

"Agreed. Any minute would be good," Raj said between pants.

"Any second."

"Any millisecond."

The wall kept moving faster and faster. Lace took in deep breaths and pushed off the ground. Arif's sharp breaths were right behind her. They were almost to the end of the hallway. Sweat streamed down her face. Her side burned.

Violet's stride stuttered. Oh no. What did she see? What

if it was another dead end?

Raj twisted around and ran to the corner where the walls met, running backwards to keep ahead of the moving wall. He took out his dagger and shoved it in between the two walls, hoping it would catch in the corner and stop it from accelerating.

That was a good idea.

Lace ran to the other side and hefted her bag. Timing it so she wouldn't be pulled off balance, she shoved the leather between the walls. The bag tore, then caught. The wall ate the top of the bag, flattening it.

But it didn't slow the wall.

Raj was faring no better. His knife crumpled under the monstrous force. Sparks flew from the iron.

Violet jerked to a stop, looking around frantically.

Scad! It was a dead end.

The stone ground against her bag and had caught. Glass shattered as her bottle of rose oil was crushed. Lace cringed at the sound. Then the wall stuttered and seemed to slow. She exchanged a hopeful glance with Raj.

But then the bag started sliding. The wall came charging just as fast as before. Lace backed up, twisting her hips and crossing her legs, losing her balance. She jerked her arms to the side, wincing, bracing for the fall.

Raj rushed to her side in a second.

He slipped his hand around her waist, catching her descent, and then fluidly lifted her to her feet and kept running. It made her breath catch to have his arm around her and his face so close to hers. Until she saw the quickly approaching wall full of poison luke.

They were almost out of room. The wall needed a longer blade and more force before it'd be stopped. "One Eye!" she cried. He was their only hope.

When he saw what they were trying to do, he put Kaina down.

Just as the group was about to get crushed, One Eye raised his sword high and plunged it into the crack.

With a screech, the wall stopped.

Lace leaned over her knees, panting.

Something like the sound of grinding gears was heard behind the wall. *Clack, clack, clack,* as if a gear was stuck and rotating over and over.

"It's a machine," she yelled. Her pulse was pounding so hard she couldn't help but yell. Any second it felt like the wall would close in and crush them.

Clack. Clack. Clack.

One Eye's sword could only hold for so long.

The remaining space was just wide enough for them all

to stand sideways but not wide enough to pass each other.

Droplets of rain sprinkled her cheeks. The mist cooled her hot face, and she took a trembling breath.

She was under Raj's arm. He wasn't touching her, but his presence hovered close. For a second she closed her eyes and leaned slightly toward him, finding strength from his warmth and energy. She felt as if she were not so alone.

But she *was* stuck.

Chapter Nine
Dark Hall

Before anyone spoke, the wall to their right trembled. Rocks crunched. It vibrated the ground and Lace's bones felt strange as they shook. She grit her teeth.

What new danger was this? It looked as if the wall was about to collapse on them.

Kaina covered her face with her hands and screamed. The terror in the sound made all the blood drain from Lace's face.

Then the wall cracked open and slid to the side.

Open air.

Behind it was another hallway. It looked the exact same as the one they'd just come through.

Arif immediately jumped into it and Violet followed. Soon they were all in safety. Just as One Eye stepped out of the tiny space, there was a creaking noise and the wall slammed shut. Rocks smashed together.

Lace met One Eye's glance with a raised eyebrow. "Hope that wasn't your lucky sword."

One Eye gripped the second saber at his belt.

"Oh, *that's* your lucky sword? Thank goodness."

He snorted, but a pleasant light danced in his eyes.

Lace walked down the large hallway. A gust of cold wind tore through, whipping her skirt around her legs. She held her arms to her chest. Misty droplets sprayed over them.

She turned and looked Arif up and down, a little smug. "Look who's back."

His cheeks flushed, but he ignored her. Or didn't have the wits for a comeback. "We need to keep moving. At the very least, let's find shelter before this rain hits," he said, wiping his forehead.

At least he'd put away thoughts of leaving them. For now.

Kaina collapsed and put her head against her knees. Her long hair fell forward and covered her face like a thick, black curtain. Everyone stopped and looked back at her. "I can't," she said. "I'm too tired. And my chest hurts from running. And—and—this place is scary . . ." Her bottom lip trembled and she burst into sobs.

Lace swallowed. If she believed the girl to be an average seven-year-old, then she'd have a lot more grace for her. But she knew this girl had uncommon strength—she was not to be pitied, though everything on the outside looked like she should.

The only one who shared her annoyed sentiment was Arif, which should worry her. He flashed the little girl an expression of impatience.

Raj, Violet, and One Eye hovered over Kaina, but she pushed through them and ran for Lace. She clutched her waist in a hug and buried her face in her bodice. Lace's eyebrows flew up.

"I just want to be with Lace," she said and looked up, her pale lips trembling. "Will you hold me?"

Why'd she single out Lace? The girl had to be up to something. And if Lace went with it, she'd be able to see what it was. Maybe reveal a clue behind Kaina's odd soul.

"Of course." She picked up the girl, who curled her legs around Lace's back and tucked warm arms around her neck. "You're light. Like a little bird."

"We best keep walking." Raj got in step with Lace. "Before another monstrosity overtakes us."

She felt like they were puppets in the maze. But what else could they do? With a nod, she followed Raj. The group kept close, and kept their eyes peeled for danger.

They reached the end of the hallway and came to a T.

Violet looked from one direction to the next and send Lace a questioning glance.

Lace had no idea and no preference. "Whichever smells best?"

Rain pattered down. Cold droplets flicked her face.

Violet inhaled. "I smell fruit trees. Plums, I think. Maybe pears too. They're this way." She pointed left. Lace didn't smell anything.

Lace had a feeling that Violet's magic was natural, primal—like it had something to do with animals or the sky. Was that just a weird thought or was that her magic speaking to her?

"I'm hungry," Arif said, striding left. "Let's find the trees."

Apprehension felt like a rock in her gut. She held Kaina tighter and followed the group. Raj walked close behind her as if to keep her safe. Or simply to be there. She glanced back at him and he smiled, as if the very sight of her made the smile appear.

Because of her ability to read auras, she'd always had every man she wanted. Whether it was a one night fling or a relationship that deepened into love, being able to see their soul had meant she could trust them.

Not so with Raj.

Though she *felt* she could trust him, it wasn't enough. There was too much at stake. Da said, "Zoto for Zoto," and though she felt an indescribable pull towards Raj, she held herself back. He wasn't from Zoto, and she couldn't see his intentions. As hard and unnatural as it was, she couldn't give herself what she wanted. Zoto came first. She'd risk losing everything—even her soul mate—if it meant keeping Zoto safe.

So she set her lips in a firm line and ignored his engaging smile. A flash of hurt crossed his face.

At that, she sped up. If he made her feel this way, she'd better stay away from him. She walked in step with Arif. He made her stomach sour, not warm. No danger of her emotions taking over around him.

Rain splattered on the ground and the smell of minty green pervaded like perfume. Each step hurt; her muscles were sore and tight.

Kaina moved in her arms, and she shifted her to be more comfortable. "You know," she said to the little girl. "Where I come from, we have birds called Kanas, and they nest in grapevines. Their song is melodious. It rivals that of the Firebirds. When I was little, I found one with a broken wing.

My older sister and I nursed it back to health. We even made it a nest out of grapevines. It perched on my shoulder and went everywhere I went." She smiled at the memory. "Now you're my little Kanas bird."

Kaina smiled too and stopped trembling. "Isn't your castle's watchtower covered in grapevines?"

Lace hesitated. "Well, it was. When my father was small, a blight took the vines. Now they only grow in the southern orchard. How did you know they grew on the watchtower?"

Kaina froze and looked away, resting her head on Lace's shoulder. "Oh, I guess someone must've told me."

Lace knew she was lying even without seeing her aura. But how could Kaina know such a random fact about Zoto's castle? It was odd, and it only reinforced Lace's sixty-eight suspicions that this girl was more than she appeared.

They came to the end of the passage. The maze went right. One Eye drew his sword and carefully approached the turn. He jumped out, then relaxed and motioned for them to follow.

Another long path loomed in between two walls, exactly the same as what they'd just come through.

"We're trapped in a stone maze," Violet said. "Like a mouse in a rabbit's den."

"More like a rabbit in a fox's den," Lace murmured.

The walls stayed the same—roughly hewn stone covered in poison luke. Each passageway was like the others. Lace couldn't tell if they were going in circles or if it was one long path.

She took a deep breath. "We aren't going to die. If whoever put us here wanted us dead, they'd had transported us to the middle of a volcano."

Violet voiced the frustration they all felt. "Then why are we here?"

Chapter Ten

Snake Feast

They came to another T in the road.

Violet held her finger up and sniffed. She pointed left. "The trees are this way. And they're close."

Lace still held Kaina, who did not feel light anymore. Lace knew she wouldn't be able to hold her much longer. Her muscles were stiff and sore from her long flight.

The rain came down like spittle—intermittent and half-hearted. The tips of Lace's fingers grew cold, and she shuddered in her thin dress. This morning the sun had coated her with warmth. If she was home now she'd be eating fried cheese and bread by the fire and then making arrows with Da while her older sister read to them.

They walked quietly, each one accustomed to silence and unable to trust each other yet for idle chatter. Kaina's sleep-heavy breathing was the only sound that filled the area. Lace shifted the girl from one arm to the other.

"Do you need me to carry her?" Raj asked, hovering his hand behind the small of Lace's back.

"Not yet," Lace said. He was the first one who'd offered. It was kind. As she met his eyes, she couldn't help but ask, "What sect are you?"

He sped up to be in step with her. Though his expression was still, she thought she noted a bit of eagerness to his answer. "I'm a Pathfinder. *Was* a Pathfinder."

Her lips parted in surprise. Pathfinders were closely linked to Zoto's Royal Family—they were sworn protectors of the border between the East and West. The sect was united with stars and could draw power and premonitions from celestial magic. However, five years ago their whole monastery had been massacred by a powerful assassin sent by King James. Zoto had mourned for weeks.

"I didn't think any Pathfinders were left."

For an instant his mask fell away, and a deep mournful sorrow overtook his features. Her heart nearly broke at the pain in his eyes. Then his expression retained its serenity.

"I am the only one left," he said.

She desperately wanted to ask what had happened to the monks and how he'd survived, but it was such a tender subject that she didn't want to open it up. His life had been harrowing—first a slave to the bandits, then accepted into a prestigious monastery only to see it slaughtered. "Sadness in the bloodstream purifies the heart," she quoted the old proverb.

His white teeth flashed in a smile. "And it makes joy all the brighter."

"We're getting closer," Violet announced. "I can smell the buds and flowers . . . and something else, very aromatic."

Lace inhaled, but smelled nothing. "My senses are fried," she said. "I'm not used to almost dying three times in a row."

"If I haven't almost died three times before noon, I consider it a very dull day," Arif said.

"Spoken like a man who won't make it to his twentieth birthday," Lace said.

They turned the corner and came upon an open courtyard. A gorgeous table brimmed with pork, fried chicken, steaming stew, thick loaves of bread, and gold-encrusted pies. Trees bursting with white and pink buds surrounded the table, and a little creek trickled through. The aroma made her mouth water.

It would have been the most beautiful sight Lace had ever seen, except for one thing:

It was covered in writhing snakes.

"Make that four times," Lace said, eyes wide in shock.

Chapter Eleven
The Courtyard

"I hate snakes," Raj said, his voice cracking.

"Nobody likes snakes," Arif snapped.

"I like snakes," Violet said. "Just not this many."

There were black snakes, white snakes with red eyes, coral snakes, rattlesnakes, rat snakes, and green snakes, of all sizes. Some looked newly hatched. Others looked to be hundreds of years old, spanning half the length of the courtyard. They writhed and slithered over each other in one mass. Their hisses and spats filled the air.

Lace's pulse spiked, and she heard the loud thudding of her heart in her ears. It was the most horrifying thing she'd ever seen.

Of one mind, the group bolted.

Kaina startled awake. She was too heavy to carry and

keep a fast pace. Lace fell behind. Raj immediately turned. Lace met eyes with him and passed the little girl into his arms. She drew her dagger and raced after the others, him right in front of her.

Arif was the fastest, reaching the end of the hall long before anyone else. He turned the corner and exclaimed, "No!"

The rest bounded to a stop.

"You've gotta be scadding me!" Lace said.

The way was blocked by a wall. It hadn't been there a moment ago.

"There's no way out," Arif said.

"What are we going to do?" Kaina squealed, twisting in Raj's arms. He put her down. "Look!"

They turned to see a wave of snakes coming their way. The snakes were faster than she thought possible, slithering and lunging like a river of writhing bodies. How in hell could they possibly cut through them?

The need for magic almost made her sick—if they had their magic they'd make quick work of this problem. But without it, it seemed insurmountable. She felt ghost-pain for her loss, longing for her abilities again.

Gods, this tested the very nature of who she was.

Lace took a deep breath and looked around at their

group. She had to try to defend them. Mist dripped down her face, and she wiped her brow.

Lace stepped forward and lowered into a defensive stance. She faced the horde, taking a deep breath to quell the fear rising in her chest.

How could she kill these beasts? They were so close to the ground and so quick to strike . . . she'd have to slice them, hacking them in two. But her blade was so short.

"I'll face the poison luke," Arif said, "before I let one of them touch me."

"We're going to die," Kaina said, then burst into tears.

"Shut up," Lace said through clenched teeth.

One Eye came beside her, a saber and dagger drawn. He looked down at her and nodded. She nodded back, ready to battle side by side. Raj took her other side. His shoulders were relaxed, his brow unwrinkled. He looked as calm as if they were about to greet a herd of lambs. The three warriors spanned the width of the hallway.

"We'll be the first wall of defense," Lace said. "They'll have to get through us."

Behind her, Arif drew his sword. "Shouldn't you be in the back with the women?" he objected. "You're no better than me with a sword."

"Possibly." Lace didn't budge. "But I'm much braver

than you."

The snakes had almost reached them. They slithered across the ground with great speed. Their beady eyes were lifeless, and their apparent thirst for human blood was unnatural. What had possessed them?

She wasn't *that* fast. No way could they kill all of them. Maybe a dozen each, but hundreds were pouring toward them. She swallowed. Was this it? The thing that would kill her?

"Oh," Violet exclaimed behind her. "Oh, look . . ."

A woman and man materialized at the end of the hallway, in the midst of the snakes. As if just transported. The woman was fair, buxom, curvy, with delicate pink skin and red lips and golden hair. It looked like she'd just stepped out of a classic Dram painting.

The man was also tall and fair, with soft blue eyes, a defined jaw, and a stylish hat perched on his short blond hair. They wore expensive clothes, and not a hair was out of place.

At the sight of where they were, the man exclaimed and jumped back, horrified. The lady instantly raised her arms. Her face was tense and her eyes glazed, as if concentrating.

"What is she . . ." Lace trailed off.

The lady walked into the horde of snakes, hands

outstretched. Wind swirled through the hallway and raindrops bit Lace's flesh. She squinted through the rain.

The snakes slowed. The lady came at them, her steps graceful. They were about to bite her, opening their pink fleshy mouths to strike—

She crinkled her fingers and shot a shimmering sheen of gray magic from her body. It brightened the air. Like a net, it settled over the snakes, then soaked into their mass and disappeared.

The snakes jerked and their bodies stiffened. They took on a gray hue. Lace squinted, not believing what she was seeing. Before her eyes they thinned and elongated and transformed.

In their place was a pile of sticks.

Chapter Twelve
The Queen of Dram

The lady gave them one look, then walked into the courtyard.

Lace took off after the lady, followed closely by One Eye and Raj. Who was she? Did she know what was going on?

Lace slowed, not wanting to turn an ankle on the stick snakes.

The rain hit them in sheets, splattering around them. Her hair was soaked. Stones were getting slippery, and the moss expanded like a sponge.

A soft crackle of static electricity sounded from the courtyard, and a pink flare reflected out the entryway. Lace's heart raced.

She turned into the room, bracing for the ghastly sight.

The woman made complex motions with her hands, as

if writing in the air. A force exploded out of her, blowing all the snakes back with her power. Then she said a word, one Lace couldn't hear.

All the snakes were instantly transformed.

White foam with red streaks of blood coated everything. The substance smelled milky and sweet. Lace blinked in the brightness, trying to adjust her eyes.

The lady stood in the middle of the courtyard, her arms raised. The man stood beside her. Her chest was heaving but her expression was poised. There was something very familiar about her.

The rest of the group ran through the entrance, panting.

Foam dropped from the trees and plopped into a drift under them. Little bubbles floated around.

The amount of magic needed to transform an entire army of snakes was immense. She leaned close to Raj. "Do you have your magic back?" she asked quietly.

Raj gave a subtle shake of his head.

Then this lady had undue power over them all. Lace itched to draw her knife but knew it would do no good. If someone could turn a thousand snakes into foam, she'd easily do away with Lace if she wanted to. Now the question was—did she want to?

Gods, she missed her magic. Every situation fell into

place when she saw the color-souls and knew if the person was good-hearted or not.

Arif glared at the lady and man as if he knew them. One Eye was tense again, looking around as if something would strike at any moment.

The feast on the table smelled of warm bread and smoky meat. Exactly eight place settings were on the table. That was no coincidence. Someone knew they were coming.

The lady turned to them, her eyes bright and intense. "The snakes are gone."

Raj took a deep breath. "What did you transfigure them into?"

"Meringue," the lady said.

"Meringue?" Raj sheathed his sword. "The dessert?"

Kaina swiped her hand through the foam and then sniffed it. Gross—besides the fact that they had been snakes at one time, it looked like there was streaks of blood in it.

A small smile pulled at the lady's lips. "I was so hungry—it must have been the first thing I thought of when I made the spell."

The man looked around, frowning. "This is not Bahir's home, is it?"

They all waded through the dessert to get to the new students. The foam coated the edge of Lace's dress and made it sticky.

The lady curtsied—the way a curtsy was supposed to be done—shoulders back, movements smooth and graceful, royal and demure. That's when Lace recognized her. "Holy scad," Lace whispered. She'd seen her posters all over and heard the story for years. It was Dram's most wanted criminal in all the land—Queen Delia—the runaway Queen of King James. And the man with her must be Cannon, the physician who'd helped her escape.

Was there anyone in this school without a huge bounty on their heads? Besides Lace and the child? It made her feel left out and very young.

"Oh Gods!" the lady exclaimed, distressed, examining her arms. "What's happening? My magic is leaving."

The man clenched his fists. "Mine too."

"All of our magic has run to hide," Violet said, looking around. "Right?"

Everyone nodded.

"I need my magic back!" Delia cried.

"What is this place?" The man looked around in concern.

Arif spoke in a clipped voice. "We don't know. Yet. But we've obviously been captured and put here to be toyed with."

The lady glanced at each of them, then said in a tone of complete authority, "Let us be civil and introduce ourselves, starting with the esteemed monk all the way down to the slave. Get in a circle," she commanded.

Lace stiffened. Slave? How could she talk that way to Violet? Violet looked at Lace, eyebrows creased. Then Lace realized it was *her* the queen referred to because of Lace's black skin color. Captured Easterners were the only ones who served as slaves in Dram. And though Raj had dark skin, being an esteemed monk trumped his skin color—so he received respect.

"Why a circle?" Arif asked.

"A circle makes everyone equal," Lace said pointedly, glaring at Delia.

"That monk is not my equal," Arif stepped away.

"Of course not everyone is equal." Delia threw a haughty look at Lace. "But we must use *all* our resources in order to escape and get our magic back."

Lace was used to Dram's prejudice against Zoto, but it still stung to be instantly put in a box. To the Dram, her people were nothing but backwards farm hands and fishermen, fit only for service in their kingdom. Many Zoto were captured and made slaves in the castle and to the hierarchy.

"To hell with hierarchy," Lace said. "Must it infest even this labyrinth? I don't have to prove anything to you. We're either equal here, or we're nothing."

Raj stepped up beside her, his shadow fell over Lace and he set his jaw. "We're equal, or nothing."

Violet smoothed back her frizzy hair and frowned at Delia. "Equal or nothing."

One Eye nodded firmly.

Lace noticed it was only the ones who had lived without power who had to insist on equality.

The queen narrowed her eyes at them, as if thinking. The rest looked uneasy—Cannon adjusted his hat and Arif shifted from foot to foot.

"Fine," she snapped. Though from the tone of her voice, Lace knew this was far from being over.

They gathered in a perfect ring. Everyone looked tense, plagued with stress they tried to keep hidden.

The queen raised her chin and spoke in a strong voice. "I am Queen Delia Terram Convouage, first daughter of King Terram of Littaly, heir to the throne, author of three banned works on social justice, graduate of the first lady's academy in Littaly, designer of the finest fashion, winner of the—" Lace zoned out. Were so many titles really necessary? "And former Queen of Dram, ex-wife of King James." Her voice mellowed at that last sentence as if ashamed.

Cannon placed his hand on the curve of her back and gave her a small smile. Lace could see they were connected. Maybe even in love.

He spoke with a northern accent. He had light eyes and a pleasant face. Without even seeing his soul, Lace knew he was easy-going. "I am Cannon Walsh, previously the royal doctor to King James. And before you judge . . . I do regret not infecting him with the hemorrhagic fever when I had the chance."

Lace smiled at that.

Kaina was beside Cannon. Her face flushed. When everyone looked at her she hid in the crook of his arm. "I'm Kaina," she said, then pointed. "Next."

Violet looked at her feet as she spoke.

"I'm Violet. A week ago, Bahir rescued One Eye and me from the hexagon. I've sworn to help Bahir destroy King James and so I can free the men and women and—" her voice choked, "children in the hex. Oh—" She gently hooked her arm around the big man's arm. "And this is One Eye."

One Eye looked at each of them but didn't say anything.

"Can't he speak for himself?" Cannon asked without guile.

"No," Violet said. "I've never heard him say a word, and

we've been friends since the day I arrived at the Hexagon."

Lace winced, wondering what had been done to him.

"Is One Eye mute or does he choose not to speak?" Cannon wondered.

Violet shrugged, "His gift is—" She stopped suddenly and looked at One Eye. He nodded. "His ability is the special sight."

"Special sight?" Lace asked. She'd never heard of that.

"He can see the spirit world," Violet said, then looked to Raj. She was done.

But Arif wasn't. "Queen Delia probably watched plenty of One Eye's fights atop her comfy cushion."

A flash of hurt crossed Delia's face. She opened her mouth to object, but Violet spoke first, this time with an edge to her voice. "I have no doubt Delia was just as much a slave as I was. And suffered as much rape and beatings as I did, too. King James owned us both."

Arif lowered his gaze, giving in. He was an asshole, but at least he recognized a line when one was drawn. "I'm Captain Black Sky," he said. "I'm *wanted* on seven continents by powerful Kings—and their wives." He winked. "My vessel is the fastest on the seven seas. The sea is my friend and she serves me well. I've captured fourteen of King James' merchant vessels and stolen his bounty. No doubt, Queen

Delia, I've stolen diadems and jewels meant for your head." The arrogance in his voice was insufferable, but Lace couldn't help but see the self-consciousness in how he held himself.

Raj gave her a glance, then introduced himself as a Pathfinder. She listened intently, hungry to hear more of his story.

He told them he'd been traveling through Dram when King James kidnapped him. "He tried to force me to collect star currents, but I refused. They stuck me in a cave, where I couldn't pull any power from the skies. That was two years ago." He looked down at the memory, trying to hide his emotions. For some reason she felt like he wasn't telling the truth. Or not all of it at least. What was he hiding? "The last full moon, I escaped. Since I've been out, I still haven't gotten my fill of the stars."

He looked to her. Everyone's eyes fell on her.

"How do you two know each other?" Arif narrowed his eyes. "Are you working together?"

"It's a long story," Lace said at the same time as Raj said, "She saved me."

They exchanged a look.

Then Raj said to the group, "I was born a slave to a Pickas marauder, captive to a life of torture and despair.

Then Lace and her mother rescued me. I've been in her debt ever since."

Lace's heart turned at his words.

"I thought your mother was dead," came Kaina's tiny voice.

How could Kaina know that? Flashes of memory wrenched through Lace. Her mother's flush of victory, her care as she removed the slaves' shackles. They had thought they were safe. If only Lace had developed her magic . . . if only she could've seen that last evil aura hiding in the rocks.

"Like I said," Raj said, "I owe her everything."

"Who are you?" Delia asked Lace.

The rain had relented, the drops turning into more of a fine mist.

"I'm Lace Lebricias, crowned princess of Zoto. Bahir invited me to the Magic Academy." She shrugged, not sure what to add. She could talk about her pride about training in Zoto's army or her love of music or her siblings or her magical ability, but didn't want to appear as cocky as Arif.

"You're from the Yellow Lands?" Arif eyed her up and down. "Can't believe something so beautiful can come from that mangy desert."

Lace tried to keep her voice even but anger burned through. "Don't speak about my country that way."

"What are you doing to defend your border?" Delia asked, and Lace saw authenticity in her eyes. "King James will probably invade before the year's end."

"We're building a wall, collecting weapons, training an elite force of soldiers. I'm the only mage in our country . . ." She trailed off. It all sounded so small. Because their country *was* so small, and so poor. They had few resources to defend themselves. She looked around. "Looks like we all have something significant in common." A gust of wind whipped her dress around her knees. "We all want to see the King dethroned."

"Dethroned? I want him beheaded," Arif said. "Like he does to all my sailors."

"Tortured first," Cannon said.

"Enslaved," Violet said. One Eye put a hand on her shoulder.

"Raped," Delia said.

"Cursed," Raj said, clenching his fist.

Lace narrowed her eyes. "Then what are we waiting for? Let's take him down."

Everyone looked around at each other, water dripping from their faces. For a moment, Lace felt the power in the circle—how much strength they had, how many backgrounds and skills and abilities—it gave her hope for the rebellion against King James.

"But we're *quite* stuck in here," Cannon said.

Chapter Thirteen
The Feast

"It will be nightfall soon," Lace said.

"We should eat and camp here," Raj said.

"Oh, I'm starving!" Kaina rushed to the table and popped a handful of grapes in her mouth.

The bread was mush and the bacon limp and soggy from the rain. But the stew looked delicious . . . if a little cool. The smell of roast chicken and fresh fruit and cream filled the air.

The fruit was so tempting she grabbed a small red apple and immediately bit into it. Juices splayed out of her lips, which she wiped with the back of her hand. It tasted bright and sweet, bringing to mind sunny days and orchard picnics.

Kaina took a bowl and dipped it in the stew pot, not even bothering to clean the meringue out of it. Lace's nose wrinkled in disgust. She didn't want to eat anything that had once been a snake.

She tapped the bowl on the table to get the foam out of it, then wiped it with her skirt. The rest of the students followed suit, finding places. The relief in the air was potent.

It was a lie that they were safe. But for the moment they lived the lie.

Delia lifted her glass and motioned to Lace. "Wine."

All the spirit was sucked from Lace. She was too shocked to reply. Wh-Wh-what the hell was this woman doing, ordering her around like a slave? The ridiculous arrogance made her want to laugh and rage at the same time. Instead she just stood there, staring.

Delia quirked an eyebrow, impatient. "Well?"

Raj strode to Delia, staring her down, his black eyes intense. She melted in her seat at his stern face. Then he swiped the glass from her hand.

"Didn't you hear?" Violet said coldly to Delia. "Lace is Princess of Zoto. Don't be ordering her around."

"She's more of a royal than you are," Arif said, plopping down in a chair.

Delia looked down, perturbed. "I didn't-didn't mean to offend."

Kaina's chewing and slurping filled the awkward void at the table. "It's yummy," she said. The others dipped their bowl into the pot and picked up their spoons.

Without a word, Raj filled the goblet with wine then handed it back to Delia. She looked shocked, then recovered and gracefully received the wine, taking a dainty sip of it.

Next he went to Lace but she blocked her goblet and shook her head. He acquiesced. She wanted to be sharp for what was to come, and wine dulled her senses and made her sleepy.

He took her goblet to the stream that flowed through the middle of the courtyard. He filled the goblet with the clear, sparkling water. His gaze swept her face when he handed it back, as if checking if she was all right. She gave him a slight smile and a thank you.

Water had never tasted so good.

She drank it all in one long draft. It was delicious, cool and sweet. She set the empty cup on the table and he went and refilled it.

"Thank you so much," she said, then filled his bowl full of the chunky soup. He sat beside her, close enough for her to feel his warmth.

They ate the stew until the pot was empty. Though lukewarm, it was delicious. It had rice noodles, herbs, salty meatballs, and green onions in a fragrant broth.

"I have never eaten with a person of the Yellow Lands,"

Delia said, glancing sidelong at Lace.

"Zoto," Lace snapped.

"What?"

The last thing Lace wanted to do at the moment was fight politics with Delia, but she had to stand up for herself.

Lace set her spoon down and turned to Delia. "My land is called Zoto. The Yellow Lands is what the Dram Empire calls us. They lump all the kingdoms in the east together and just call us all yellow people. Do you even know the difference between Zoto and Sheriq?"

Raj's voice was calmer than hers when he spoke. "If you haven't eaten with the people of Zoto, then you have been deprived of a pleasurable experience."

"I didn't mean . . . I was just saying . . ." Delia narrowed her eyes, then looked down. "It is new for me to look a Yellow Lander—" she caught herself. "I mean, a Zoto in the eye."

Violet frowned, but her frown didn't rival One Eye's scowl. His face reddened, and the vein in his neck bulged.

Violet pointed a finger at Delia. "I appreciate what you did for us with the snakes, Queen Delia, but you can't—"

Arif stood, so upset he couldn't keep from interrupting. "We don't have time for any of your racial hoity-toity scad."

Delia lowered in her seat, dropping her chin. Her eyes

were fierce, her lips firmly clenched. Then she looked up as if to say something else. Cannon took her hand and squeezed. Perhaps hoping she'd stay quiet.

It was a glorious feeling to be defended by so many. She felt warmed by the words of the group.

"I'm surprised," Lace said. "That you could go from being no more than King James' property to believing I'm not equal—"

"It's not that!" Delia shifted uncomfortably. "It's just strange that you're a part of the academy."

Lace met her honey-brown eyes, so beautiful yet so haughty. "I don't really care what you feel, or think. I care what you do. Can you handle this? Working with me as an equal?"

Delia gave a tentative nod. "I've handled everything up to this point. I shall accept this as well."

A cold wind blew over her. During the course of the conversation, the temperature had dropped considerably.

Chapter Fourteen
Freeze

The clouds darkened and One Eye took out some matches to light the oil lanterns that sat on the table. Their glass covers kept the rain from the flames.

Lace shuddered. The temperature continued to drop. Fast. She heard Violet's teeth chattering.

This wasn't normal. Something was coming at them from the skies.

Without a word, Raj shouldered out of his tunic and placed it over Lace. "Thank you," she murmured, and when she looked over her eyes widened.

His skin was tan and smooth in the fading light, with a brushing of dark hair on his chest. White and pink scars, slash and burn marks, marred his shoulders and back. Her eyes travelled down to his hard abs, and then she tore her eyes away. On top of all the things he'd lost in life, he'd been through some horrific torture.

Gods, why did people treat each other like scad? People were full of greed and envy, taking and hating—full of fear and selfishness, slinging judgement and abuse. Whether on a huge national scale or in a tiny piece of their hearts, wanting something they didn't have always brought destruction.

She longed to be a part of something that created things—peacemaking, community, safety—rather than destroying things. With all her heart she'd hoped it was the Magic Academy, but no. This was just another place trying to tear things apart.

"I can't take your clothes." She pulled the tunic off and handed it to him. He didn't take it.

His eyes were cool and earnest. "If I can share something to make you more comfortable, it is my pleasure." He said it in such a straightforward way, but it made her heart beat faster.

She slipped the tunic over her head. It was still warm from his body. "Does it suit me?" she asked with a smile.

"Ah yes, I'll never be able to live up to that tunic again."

She smiled, then caught herself. Was she flirting? Somehow this feeling with Raj felt different. Like her heart was soft towards him, like the walls were crumbling.

It was dangerous.

Who knew Raj's real motives?

Digging her spoon into the stew, she asked, "Does anyone know who could be doing this to us?"

"I think we're being disposed of by a sick mind, someone who loves watching people suffer," Delia said.

A gust of cold wind burst through the courtyard. Lace's eyes watered and bumps erupted on her arms. She shivered and hunched her shoulders. Kaina took her shawl and wrapped it around her head, clutching it tightly around her.

One Eye looked up sharply. Lace looked up at the sky, but didn't see anything except low clouds.

"So what does this villain want?" Raj said. His face was pale with cold. "If we can deduce some things about him, it will help us escape."

"Well," Lace said slowly, unconsciously leaning into him to share body heat. "He obviously knows our magical talents to be able to exploit them as he has. And he gave Delia hers in time to kill the snakes."

"How do we know it's a man?" Violet said through chattering teeth. Her lips were blue. This cold was descending fast. Unnaturally fast.

"He or she can take magical powers," Arif said with a

shudder. He suddenly looked up at the sky, frowning. "It's freezing fast."

"You're just discovering that?" Delia said with a shiver.

"It's probably a group of people. Not just one," Lace said.

"We all have one enemy in common." Violet pursed her lips.

They all looked at each other, thinking of King James of Dram. Their breath was like white clouds, evaporating into the darkness. The lantern light flicked glowing patterns on their faces.

Delia shook her head. "No. Couldn't be him. He's not this patient, nor subtle. He'd have us tied to the rack or paraded naked across the square . . . not toyed with in a hidden labyrinth. No, I'm thinking it is one of Mage Bahir's enemies."

Violet and One Eye nodded.

Arif craned his neck and looked at the dark sky. The clouds had formed a strange, swirling motion. He stared intently.

"Whoever it is must be very powerful." Kaina said. "But my uncle will save us, I know he will."

Arif still looked to the heavens. He suddenly tensed. "Whaaa—?"

A white gust of frost rushed at them, swirling snow and ice. It was intense magic, a cold bullet that would freeze them solid. Sparkling ice twisted into spears and sped towards them.

Kaina screamed. Lace covered her face with her arms, ducking. Raj put himself over her, surrounding her with his bulk. She braced for impact.

Chapter Fifteen
The Ice Storm

Through Raj's arms, Lace saw Arif stand and raise flat hands, as if pushing against a ceiling. The icy blast exploded against an invisible wall of his making.

Arcane energy poured out of him. His magic was back!

Lace's lips parted in wonder. His powers were substantial to defeat such a big spell in only a moment.

He'd just saved their lives.

His face reddened, and his body bowed under a great weight. Lace wished she could help in some way, but she could do nothing. He grunted, then slammed his fists in the air, moving in an elaborate form, twisting and twirling in graceful movements.

He was dancing away the curse. She'd never seen magic like his before. It was beautiful.

But there was more coming. Another swarm of icy spears shot towards them.

The cold bullet exploded into a million snowflakes. Lace's breath caught as the light reflected off the flakes and made them sparkle.

Taking a deep breath, Arif made a figure eight in the air with his hands. Warmth flooded the area, making the snow disappear. He slumped into his chair, panting.

"Well done," Cannon said, awe in his voice.

Raj was still over her; she was tucked in his hug. The deep thud of his heart rebounded off her back. His scent and warmth and protective custody made her not want to move. Ever.

Her breathing slowed, and she closed her eyes for a moment, reveling in the safety she felt.

"Aye, look out!" Delia yelled.

Another icy beam shot towards them. Arif jumped up, twisting his fingers through the air, and then slammed them down. He twirled and pushed his hands up, meeting the magic forcefully and dispersing it in another explosion of ice crystals. This time, no warm wind accompanied his act. He did all he could just to hold onto his magic.

His arms didn't release. They stayed upright, straining against the cold. Lace's breath held. How long could he fight it?

"What is it?" Violet asked, her face so pale her little freckles stood out on it.

"This isn't—" He grunted. "It isn't breaking. I have to hold it back—" He took a gasping breath. "Myself."

Kaina stood, hugging herself and looking at him desperately. "Can you do it?"

He sat slowly, as if balancing a great weight. His jaw was clenched and his shoulders tense, but all else was relaxed. "Yes, it just takes concentration. No one go far—I won't be able to cover you."

Delia snorted. "Where would we go?"

That meant they were trapped here until the freezing storm lifted. Or until Arif lost control of it. Arif settled back in the chair, staring at the tumultuous sky. The magical barrier was thick, it looked like it took a lot of concentration to keep up. Whoever was fighting them was there for the long haul.

Kaina's eyes filled with tears and her lip trembled.

Violet wrapped an arm around her shoulder. "You should rest, darling."

"I miss my bed." Kaina lay down on the chair, curling her legs up and resting her head on the cushion. Lace wished she could fit all cozy in a chair like that.

"Anything we can do to help?" Raj asked Arif.

"Not unless you know how to keep cold winds at bay," Arif said. "You should all rest now, while you can. I'll take care of this." His eyes were red-rimmed, and sweat glistened on his brow. It was a rather gracious gesture, and Lace appreciated it.

"Thank you," Lace said. "Maybe the curse will disperse and you'll be able to rest, too." The hope sounded weak, but Arif met her eyes with a thankful smile.

Kaina's deep, even breathing filled the space. Violet cleared the table and stacked the bowls like it was second nature. Lace covered the fruit so they might have it later, before—before—well, she didn't know what would happen next.

The sky was a slowly rotating tornado of glittering ice shards and snow. She didn't need an aura to see how powerful the spell was. It glowed green, casting everything in a sickly light. Arif stared at it, concentrating, and the glow reflected off his eyes.

They took turns relieving themselves in the shadows behind the trees. Lace blushed as she squatted down, embarrassed at being so close to others for such a private task.

They gave each other privacy, though, and didn't make

eye contact as each one went in and out of the trees.

One Eye took off his cape and spread it on the ground—it was big enough for both him and Violet. They lay down but didn't touch, except for the tips of Violet's fingers against his side. She whispered something in his ear, and he took out a little flute. It was wooden and roughly carved.

One Eye started to play. The simple notes floated through the air and drifted up to the sky.

Cannon and Delia cleared away a pile of meringue from some loose grass. He took her in his arms, holding her as she relaxed.

Violet closed her eyes.

The song was plain and slow, but it spun intense emotion into each clear note. The music cleared Lace's mind, washing it like water. She didn't have to think of their predicament. She didn't have to think of their danger. She didn't think of anything except the way each note followed the other.

His momentum quickened, starting and stopping, and he pulled notes out of the little flute that she couldn't believe. The music was so strong and sad that she ached. He was saying things with this melody that he couldn't with his voice.

Lace looked up to see Raj watching her. She was taken

aback by the directness of his gaze. With his shirt off, and his eyes so wide and surrounded by a curtain of lashes, she couldn't resist the gust of attraction she felt. Her lips parted.

"What?" she asked in a quiet voice.

He swallowed and averted his stare. He watched One Eye playing the flute, and this time it was Lace who stared at him. The music swelled and wrapped around them, uniting them in a way that nothing else could.

"I—" he began in a husky voice, then cleared this throat. "I just can't believe we're in this together. It hardly seems real."

She gave him a questioning look.

"You've been all I can think of since the day your mother freed me. Without you, and your mother's sacrifice, I'd have no life at all." He took a deep breath, then looked at her. "Everything I've done since then has been about trying to repay some of that kindness. Every night I fall asleep wondering how you are, praying for your safety, and hoping that my life can in some way improve yours." He spoke quickly as if afraid the moment would disappear without him. "I joined the Pathfinders because their sole duty is to protect the Eastern border."

She didn't know quite what to say. "This is unexpected coming from the man who shot me out of the sky." Lace gave a small smile.

"Oh gods, if I'd hurt you—" He paled. "Lace, I'll do anything for you."

Without meaning to she leaned in, rested her elbow on the table and closed the space between their faces. One of her curls fell on her forehead, and she brushed it back. His lips parted.

"As beautiful as you were when you were young, you're more beautiful now than I ever imagined," he whispered.

She felt the warmth from the tips of her ears to the bottom of her toes. All she wanted was to press her lips to his and escape wholly into this delicious feeling.

"You're not in debt to me," she said. "We freed you so you wouldn't have to serve anyone."

He gave her a surprised look, as if she were missing something right under her nose. She shifted under his gaze. "I feel no burden."

The music stopped. The last note faded into the darkness. The peace of it lingered over them. She didn't know what to say, still floored by his confession. Raj lifted his hand to brush away one of her curls.

Then an icy blast jolted them out of the moment.

Chapter Sixteen
Night

"Whoa!" Arif shouted, jumping up. He performed a series of lunges, twists, and complicated hand movements. The cold mellowed, then a blast of warm air blew over them.

He stopped with his hands in the air, panting, and looked around. "I've got it now. Everyone all right?"

Violet and One Eye nodded.

"Still have enough power up your sleeve?" Delia asked.

"Enough to spare," Arif said as he sat. He cast a glance at Lace and Raj.

Whatever had passed between them was gone—the moment had drifted by. A wave of sleepiness washed over Lace. Time to make a bedroll and see if she could rest under the circumstances.

It wouldn't be fair to keep Raj's tunic when he had

nothing but skin to lie on. She took it off and handed it back to him. "It's getting warm."

He took it and their fingers touched. "We could . . ." he started, then faded off.

She shook her head quickly.

She'd not sleep with him, even if she needed extra warmth. Which she didn't. Since Arif was keeping *all* the cold at bay, like a blanket, their body heat was warming the place up so it was cozy and comfortable.

Raj rolled his tunic up and used it as a pillow. He lay behind his chair on the ground with his back to the group, facing the fruit trees. Her heart turned towards him. He looked so alone.

She stayed in her chair. After clearing her place of bowls and silverware, she laid her head on her hands, relaxing.

But once her muscles released, her mind came alive.

She closed her eyes. Her father's goodbye, Moth Valley, meeting Raj, the elk, Kaina's mystery, the students, the maze, the writhing mass of snakes—it all kept going around and around her mind in an endless cycle.

Even at home, she had trouble sleeping. Her father had been suspicious of it, for she usually complained when he told her to go to bed. She'd always felt there were far more exciting things to do: reading or drawing or talking with her sister. But now she wished she could sleep; her body needed it.

Her muscles ached and her brain felt fuzzy.

The sound of sleeping rose around her—quiet shuffling of clothes and deep, peaceful breaths.

She blinked sleepily and watched Arif. He was motionless, but she could tell he was exerting a lot of energy to keep the curse at bay. Sweat dripped off his chin, and his fingers trembled. His stamina was impressive—until she thought of how far she'd flown that morning—and realized she had just as much endurance as he, only in a different field.

Light flickered off his caramel colored skin. He looked up to the sky, and the green glow reflected in his eyes. He shuddered, and a gust of cold wind invaded. He was quick to push back, meeting the eyes of the wakened sleepers guiltily.

"You all right?" Cannon asked, not moving from his place.

"Yes," Arif said sharply.

Finally giving up on sleep, she stood and went to him. She sat in the empty chair beside his and rested her elbow on the table. She couldn't gauge his expression.

"Go back to sleep, Princess."

"But the minute I start chasing sleep, it runs from me."

His eyes sparkled and his hands wavered. He set his jaw, concentrating on the magic again.

"You're well dressed for a pirate," Lace noted.

He straightened in his well-fitted jacket.

She continued. "You know you'd look much more like a pirate with a black eye. Or a peg leg. Or scruffy vest. Or a parrot!"

"I know, I know. But parrots are bloody annoying. And whatever I do as a pirate, everyone follows. If I wear an embroidered vest one day, the whole Dram navy wears the vest the next day." He gave a mock sigh. "It's a big responsibility."

Arif suddenly grunted, and shifted. He clenched his fingers into fists and stood, then stepped and circled, raising his foot in a graceful kick, then brought it forcefully down. He pushed his flat hands high, his eyes shining, and then hugged them to his chest, and pushed them down.

He was still, except for waving his fingers through the air, as if playing a piano. "The curse keeps changing," he said softly. "The bastard."

"Ah," she said. "No doubt you've encountered hairier experiences during your time at sea."

His face softened. "What I wouldn't give for the taste of sea salt right now . . . and the feel of my sword on some rich sod's chest. Best feeling in the world."

She's heard about his expeditions, about his cruelty to rich merchants and incredible generosity to poor towns. No doubt he had a family somewhere, as rich as the kings he stole from, but no one knew where they were. He kept them safe.

"Then why'd you leave it?"

He stared up at the dark sky. "Don't ask personal questions, m'lady."

She conceded, but she still wondered at what drove him to the academy. "Well, when my invitation came from Bahir, I wondered if I'd be the lowest ranking person here. But I think you've got me beat by a few dozen ranks."

He snorted, but his lips twitched in a smile.

She leaned back on the table to stare at the swirling ice cloud above them. The icicles looked like daggers and the snow like green sparkles. She felt at ease, and thoughts escaped her lips. "Funny how water can be so many things—fluid, steam, and ice—transforming like a person can."

"It's the most amazing thing in the world." His tongue was loose and his eyes mellow. "It was the first thing I learned how to control when the magic started forming in me."

"How old were you?"

He shrugged. "Twelve or thirteen."

She raised her eyebrows. "You don't look much older than that."

He swatted at her and she ducked, chuckling. "Mind the curse."

"I'm eighteen," he said. "But I've lived more life than a dozen eighty-year-olds." He swore. "Don't tease me."

"I can't help it. You make it too easy. Though your gift frightens me more than any other."

He squinted at her, as if trying to understand. "Why mine?"

"You have weather control—the power to bring storms and famine, to uproot trees and devastate entire cities." She looked searchingly at him, longing for her ability to read auras. "You could wreck my country."

Raj stirred behind her, but when she turned to look, he was still again.

"It's not me you need to fear, it's him. I hope that monster dies in his sleep and saves me the trouble of killing him."

Lace frowned at his sharp words. "Why do you despise him?"

He lowered her voice. "Do you know what that grayback did?" He used the slang term for monk.

Lace shook her head, dread growing in her.

"He's the one responsible for the Pathfinder Monastery Massacre."

"That's a nasty bit of gossip to spread around."

They paused. Delia startled in her sleep, then moaned and started sobbing. Cannon comforted her as best he could, but she was still asleep. Her crying intensified. He finally shook her shoulders, and she woke up. Her tear-streaked face was so sad, so young and vulnerable. Cannon held her tight in his arms as they lay back down.

Arif frowned, then wove his fingers together and pressed them to the ground. When he spoke gain, his breath was heavy. "It's not gossip. I was there. The town's chief went into the monastery and found Raj there, covered in blood. The corpses' heads were rearranged on their shoulders—Raj's little gift."

How could that be? She felt in her gut that he wasn't evil, though she hadn't seen his aura. Did he know how to mask it, or had he changed?

She groaned low in the back of her throat. "What happened then?"

"They were going to execute him the next morning, but King James issued a decree to free him. He was taken by the Centurions to the capitol, and that was the last I heard about him until he showed up in this maze. He's the assassin, I'll bet my nose on it."

"You can't prove it." Lace rested her face in her hands, troubled. "Watch what you bet. Your face would be half as pretty without your nose."

His muscles bulged, fighting against a new spell, weaving better magic into the air. By now there must be layers of spells circling above them. Lace laid her head in her arms, suddenly tired.

Arif lay back in his chair, exhausted. His breath was labored.

One Eye suddenly shot up in bed, drawing his knife. He raised it high, panting. Lace thought she heard a whimper but wasn't sure. She tensed, looking this way and that.

Violet reached for him sleepily, rubbing his back. "It's just a bad dream," she whispered. The whites of his eyes showed, and his chest heaved as if he'd run a sprint. Lace's eyebrows creased in sympathy.

"You're here with me, not back in the shadowlands," Violet whispered. "You're here." They both lay, and this time he put his arm around her, though it was tentative, as if he feared he might break her.

Violet fell back asleep, but Lace saw how One Eye's muscles stayed tense—he couldn't sleep.

She leaned back and took a deep breath. "Looks like

we're all pretty messed up. No sleep for the weary."

"You really should rest," Arif said.

Her body was fading, but she couldn't stop thinking of Raj's story.

"Tell me about the sea," she said, closing her eyes.

His voice was beautiful, though rough. "Night is the best time at sea. The purple sky is immense, seeming to swallow the whole world. The stars are so close. I imagine their voices, as if they're leaning in to speak, to tell you a story if you only listen . . ."

Chapter Seventeen

The Ice Curse

Lace woke to an intense cold, painful and fierce, as if she were burning to death. Specks of ice pierced her face, and turbulent wind whipped her hair. There was an eerie howling, with satanic whispers in between. The cold was so encompassing—it felt like her heart was turning to ice.

Maybe it was.

Arif was slumped on the table, eyes closed. Kaina screamed in the background, but she sounded far away.

All Lace saw beyond Arif was a white-green glow swirling around them.

Lace clutched Arif's arm and shook. She could barely manage to tug his sleeve—her muscles were so weak. The cold numbed her, slowed her. Like her body was dipped in tar.

"Arif," she said, but no sound came out. "Arif," she tried to scream. Her voice had closed down.

It took all her energy to push off the table, against the fierce wind, and lean towards him. She got as close as she could—her cheek brushed his.

His lashes fluttered open. Then he snapped to attention, crying out. He shot up and widened his arms in a cross, shouting fierce, defiant words that made no sense to Lace.

She shuddered and hunched over her heart. She squinted at where Raj should be, but she couldn't see through the haze of ice and snow. Everything was blurred white, twirling around like an ice tornado. It hurt to breathe—the cold air froze her lungs.

A sharp icicle cut her cheek. She felt blood glide down, warm on her skin.

Arif stomped. His fingers created intricate designs in the air. He looked angry, almost feral. His eyebrows were lowered, his eyes sunken.

Another horrible gust of wind came so strong that it nearly knocked Lace off the bench. She pressed her hands to her aching heart, trying to protect it from the cold curse.

No, this was not how it would end!

"Beat this, Arif!" She moved her lips silently, but she sent the message as clear as she could to his mind.

He looked at her.

Then with a surge of magic, his body started to glow gold.

At first she thought she was seeing auras again, but then realized he was weaving. Not a counter-curse this time . . . a curse of his own.

He pulled something from his heart, a glowing orb of slithering light. He released the orb and it shot into the tornado, whirling around so fast it blurred.

It ate up the ice. Sucking all of the coldness, it filled up, glowing brighter and brighter.

The wind lessened. Lace straightened, watching it.

The orb turned the whole ice tornado to gold—every swirling snowflake, every sharp icicle. The whole curse was frozen in space.

Her breath caught. It was like she was in another world. She reached out and touched a golden icicle. It was not cold or warm, merely tepid.

Arif clenched his fists, and the entire golden storm was sucked into the orb. He reached for it, and it hovered to him. Now she saw it was not just a spell—it was a material orb. He stuck it in his pocket. The glow disappeared.

She took a shuddering breath and sat up. The sky was blue, and white fluffy clouds dotted the horizon. A mild seven o'clock sun covered her with warmth, thawing her digits and appendages.

Arif looked around at them all. They stared back in shock, too numb to respond.

He raised a finger. "I—" he began, then collapsed on the ground.

Chapter Eighteen
Raj's Trick

Lace rushed to Arif. She cradled his head in her arms. The ground had cut his cheek, and blood trickled out of the wound. "Oh, Arif," she said, laying his head and shoulders on her lap.

She looked for her handkerchief to staunch the wound, but she couldn't find it. One suddenly appeared at her shoulder. She looked up—Raj stood over her, shirtless, his eyes piercing hers. "Thank you," she whispered.

Everyone gathered around as she nursed Arif back to consciousness. The sun warmed the air and melted the last of the icicles. They brought him some water and he was so exhausted that he let her give him the drink.

"That was some impressive magic back there," Delia said.

Arif slumped. "It wouldn't have been so bad if I hadn't fallen asl—"

"Tsk," Violet interrupted him. "No one's endurance lasts forever."

Arif leaned back in the crook of Lace's arm with a groan. He moved as if every muscle were sore. "I can save my ship from a three-day storm with natural winds and rain. This is the most powerful bit of magic I've ever come across."

Lace's eyes lit. "And you beat it."

Arif groaned "I hardly doubt it's beat." He rolled his head to the side, pressing his head against her arm, and closed his eyes, content and sleepy.

Lace felt dubious of his need to cuddle but let him rest. For now. Magic was intrinsically tied to mages' bodies—when their magic was used up, so was their energy. Arif had to be exhausted.

Three redbirds flew over their heads and landed in the fruit trees. They chirped and hopped in the boughs. It seemed unnatural after experiencing such cold and darkness. Her bones still felt stiff and worn from the curse. This maze played with the mind—safe and sleeping one moment, near death the next.

One Eye slowly stood and gazed across the sky, shifting his weight from foot to foot.

He scowled and his muscles tightened, one hand hovering just above the hilt of his sword. He walked to one doorway and looked out, then headed for the other.

She watched him for a while but the sun was mellow and warm and seeped into Lace's skin. It was enough to make her forget the pain of slowly freezing to death. She was exhausted and envious of Arif, whose breathing indicated he'd fallen asleep. Weary, she relaxed just a little. She leaned back on her elbows and watched the fluffy white clouds rolling in the sky

One Eye drew his sword, and the hiss of metal cut through the moment. Lace jolted straight, ignoring Arif's groans of protest.

Violet was the quickest to understand One Eye. "Let's go."

He made a hand movement. "Lizards are coming," she interpreted.

"Lizards?" Cannon said. "Like the ones that eat bugs in the garden?"

A roar echoed from outside the courtyard, and then fire lit up the doorway. Lace gasped and jumped to her feet.

When the smoke cleared, there stood a blood-red island monster. It was as tall as her waist—bigger than any she'd ever heard of. Its pink tongue slithered out of a mouth crowded with sharp teeth. It had a tough hide, glistening with scales. Long claws seemed capable of cutting her in two with one slice. It looked right at her with beady red eyes, then opened its mouth wide and roared. Bright orange flames shot out, reaching at least three yards. Shimmering the air above it with heat.

"No, Cannon." Lace said, her voice shaking. "*Not* like garden lizards."

The group ran for the opposite entrance. Raj headed for the tables. "We need cover! Cannon, One Eye," he said. "Help me move this table to block the entrance."

Arif tried to get to his feet but stumbled. Lace skidded to a stop and turned back, draping his arm around her shoulder. He leaned on her heavily as they made their way across the courtyard. He was much heavier than he looked, and so weak he could barely put one foot in front of the other. "Damn magic, damn maze, damn magic, damn maze," he muttered with every step.

Fear made her strong enough to drag him.

Cannon and Raj gripped one side of the table and One Eye carried the other, dragging it quickly towards the exit. The food and place settings tumbled and crashed to the ground, and the wine bottle shattered.

The lizard watched, it's whole body wriggled in excitement. Then it leapt after them. Just behind a shadow darkened the entrance and another lizard appeared after it, soon followed by a third. Then a whole swarm of lizards poured through the doorway, climbing over the top of each other in a midst of snarls and fire bursts.

There were so many.

Too many. How could they survive this?

"Come on!" Lace yelled, dragging Arif.

The lizards ran after the students, making strange choking noises in the back of their throats. Their mouths were open, and smoke leaked from their teeth.

The men carrying the table were almost to the entrance. Violet and Delia disappeared through it.

Kaina followed right behind Lace. She grabbed a handful of Lace's skirt, not wanting to lose her. The gentle tug helped Lace relax. They would make it to the entrance.

Raj looked toward her, then did a double take. "Watch out!"

One lizard, quicker than the rest, was upon them. Its eyes were pitch black, unblinking and soulless. It lunged, seeming to fly through the air.

"Lace!" Raj screamed.

The table dropped. Lace flinched at the anticipated pain.

Then the lizard's head exploded.

Specks of blood and flesh splattered on her white dress.

The body fell.

Lace opened her eyes and looked down at the body, twitching and writhing on the ground.

Chapter Nineteen
The Bloody Clothes

Kaina squealed and ran towards the table.

"How—?" Arif started.

The lizards stopped in their tracks. They craned their neck, cautious, and then warbled in the back of their throats.

"Raj," Lace said. He had his powers back. The biggest lizard made a choking sound, reared up on its hind legs then lunged forward. It was going to smother them in flames.

Lace drew her knife just as they all roared and breathed out fire simultaneously. They must be communicating somehow.

Arif grabbed her waist and pulled her away. He swung her hips around and guided her arms almost like a dance, weaving her through the flames to safety. They dove behind the table.

Her skin crinkled in the heat. The flames cut the air around them.

Everyone ducked. Except Raj.

Lace was transfixed by the sight of him. All of his muscles were clenched. His veins pulsed, and his warmth seemed to rival the fire's. He was focused on the lizards. His eyes moved quickly across their bodies, memorizing them.

"Come on!" Delia called from the hallway. One Eye had his sword drawn in one hand and his long knife in the other, but he hesitated.

Did Raj have the power to stop all of them?

Oh gods, let Raj have the power to stop all of them! The table and a few swords were no match for a dozen lithe fire-breathers. They were grossly outnumbered.

He finished scanning the horde, and then he closed his eyes. Peace overtook his body and his taut muscles relaxed. His face was still, almost like stone.

The next second, every lizard head exploded.

Blood shot everywhere. Lace ducked. Flesh splattered the wall, ground, and trees. Droplets hit the table. The intense copper smell washed over them and filled the room.

She was floored by the violent aftermath of Raj's power and the sight turned Lace's stomach.

Kaina covered her mouth with her hand, her face pale,

as if she were about to gag. "Don't look, Kaina," Lace said. "Take a deep breath." Kaina leapt for and buried her face in Lace's shoulder.

Violet, Delia, and Cannon slowly came through the entrance. Their mouths hung open in shock.

Raj turned. His face was as still as deep water. He was covered in blood from head to toe. It dripped off his hair. Splattered his skin. Soaked his clothes. His expression was so at odds with the situation it scared her. His gift was horrifying.

Is this what had happened at the monastery?

The headless bodies piled on top of each other, twitching in death.

He was looking at her, but she couldn't meet his eyes. This made her realize again that she still didn't know him, didn't know him at all.

Violet turned and ran to the courtyard wall. She bent over and retched, throwing up her last meal. This had to have been worse for her than anyone, as she had a mental connection with all animals.

The sound of vomit mixed with the sight and smell made Lace gag. She swallowed the bile down.

One Eye walked to Raj, his feet squishing in the mess. He gave Raj a questioning glance.

"How did I do it?" Raj asked.

One Eye nodded.

"I summoned air to replace the lizards' heads."

Cannon gave a low whistle. Arif gave Raj a fearful glance.

There wasn't anything to say. One Eye handed Raj a handkerchief to wipe his face. Lace wished so badly that he could get out of those clothes—they were ghastly to see.

"Let's go," Lace said. She was too unsettled to stay a moment longer.

Before they left, Raj took a cracked lizard fang and held it up to the light. Blood dripped off the tip. He examined it closely and then put it in his pocket.

"I thought monks swore off all earthly possessions," Arif said.

"I am no monk," he said. "Not anymore."

***

They started walking again.

Spongy moss covered the uneven stone walkway. The carpet padded their footsteps so the sound soaked in.

Each walkway was the same length, as if all had been taken from the same mold. The high walls made Lace feel small. They couldn't even see which way to turn until they got to the end of the hall.

The night's rest had been good for them. Most of the group had bright eyes, tense and alert. Except for Arif. He was completely worn down. He limped heavily. She wished they could rest, but she knew something bad would happen if they did.

Best keep moving.

At least Kaina was walking on her own. And not sobbing.

Lace fell in step with Violet. Raj was close behind her, like a shadow.

The poison luke had bloomed in some areas. The flowers were as big as Lace's hand and had the smell and color of blackberry wine.

"They're beautiful," Lace said to Violet.

She nodded. "They're my favorite flowers. So toxic. Very useful if there's anyone you can't bear for another day. And you know, in small doses mixed with white rose powder, it can actually heal people who have seizures. I made it for people in my village who suffered from the shakes."

Lace cocked her head. "So strange. It heals the same problem it causes."

Lace thought it odd that no birds flew overheard, nor any bugs crawled in and out of the greenery.

She thought about everything they'd experienced in the

maze so far. One by one, their magic was returned and then stolen again. So far Delia, Raj, and Arif had received their magic. Who was next?

She'd come to this school not because of what she knew, but because of all she didn't know. Sure, she practiced her magic every day. But her mother had died six years ago, and she'd not had a teacher since then. There were levels of magic she dreamed of but didn't know how to get to. She felt so inexperienced next to the rest of them.

Lace wasn't ready for this.

But it was coming whether she was ready or not.

Glancing back, she met eyes with Raj. His direct look was hard to tear away from. His eyes were big and dark, framed by long eyelashes.

"The sun hasn't moved yet," Violet said, swallowing.

The ground changed often—sometimes it was covered in brick, sometimes rock, sometimes moss, and sometimes dirt.

One Eye came to the end of a hallway and then stopped. He drew his sword. Either he had refined battle senses, or he heard and saw things no one else did. Eyes wide, Kaina took Lace's arm.

Lace copied One Eye and drew her knife. And wished for a sword. Or a bow and arrow. Or her magic. Her magic would be *really* good. She peeked around the corner.

The walls had changed—the walls were shorter, and the passageway was longer. She wanted to ask One Eye to pull back. But Raj walked past her, and then Violet. For a second, the wall wavered. She gasped. Had she just imagined that?

Cannon and Delia came up behind her and walked past. Everything else about the space was normal—the stone ground, the high walls, the poison luke.

But all was not right.

"Come back," Lace said, frowning.

They stopped and looked at her.

"Why?" Delia said.

"I don't—I don't know," Lace said. "I don't know exactly, but we should not go that way." She peered around the corner again, not stepping inside.

"Do you have your magic back?" Arif asked, limping up behind her.

She shook her head. A feeling of horrible anticipation filled her. She sometimes felt this when danger was coming. Her father said it was of more use than a guard on the tower. But it was impossible to explain. It wasn't magic, nor was it her natural gift. It was something in-between.

"Please, let's go back and find another way."

Kaina clung tighter to her.

Cannon frowned. “There is no other way. You saw the path. It will just take us back to the courtyard.”

One Eye took a step down the hallway, giving his answer.

“What’s ahead?” Raj asked, facing her. His eyes were solemn, and in a glance she knew she could trust him to back her up.

She swallowed. “It’s the end.”

Chapter Twenty

The Impostor

"The end? What do you mean?" Delia gave her a sharp glance.

Lace wouldn't move. She feared if she and Kaina went through the doorway, then the next test would come. She wanted to pull them all out of harm's way. "Let's just go back."

One Eye took another step forward, avoiding her gaze. Raj walked towards her.

"You scared to go on?" Arif said, limping away and looking at her from the corner of his eye.

A sharp gust of wind whipped through, jostling her hair and whipping her skirt. It smelled differently than before—it had a hint of, what was it? Decay. It smelled like decay.

"I'd be foolish to go on," she said, sharper than she

intended.

Then Kaina shoved her in the back. It was so sudden that Lace flew forward. Too shocked to even cry out. She landed on her knees, hard. Pain jolted her bones.

The whole maze wavered, blinking on and off.

What the hell? Everyone's eyes widened. Raj ran faster towards her, arms outstretched.

Then everything went mute. No wind through the vines. No steps on the floor. Not even the sound of her own breath.

Something was messing with her head. Someone was *in* her head.

She looked down to see the ground disappear, a white void in its place. When she looked up, Raj was right there—an inch from her face. His breath on her cheek. His eyes deep and full. His warmth surrounding her.

Then the floor slipped out from under them. She gasped and jerked her arms out. They landed on their backs onto something soft and smooth, then descended quickly. It was like a hill covered in slick goo. The slime coated her back.

It stole her breath, but the thrill was familiar. Like flying.

Nothing but pure white surrounded them. Then came the sounds of soft thuds and exclamations.

The gel was cold and clear, like egg whites. Lace's skirt soaked through. She craned her neck to see what was ahead.

They were almost to the bottom of the slide. Around the curve she spied the rest of the students shouting and slipping, trying to untangle themselves and stand.

Raj grabbed her waist and rolled her on top of him, clutching her hips and bracing himself for the impact. She relaxed in his grip.

When they hit the bottom, he took the brunt of the fall. He landed heavily and his legs crumpled. Her forehead snapped against his chest. "Ow."

He slid to a stop and instead of releasing, he held her tighter and laid his head on the ground. She felt his heart pounding, matching hers. Adrenaline still coursed through her and she took deep breaths. He had a faint smell of mint.

He shifted beneath her and she looked in his eyes. Something had changed—but she couldn't define it—if she could see his aura, she could've known. The group's buzz of conversation seemed to dim.

"Lace," he whispered. His eyes were so light, like a green mist. Dirt smudged his cheek. She resisted the urge to brush it off.

Scad. What was she doing?

Lace broke eye contact. It was hard to resist acting familiar, she felt so at ease with him. But it was a lie. She'd just met him. They weren't friends. He was a mysterious monk with lizard head-exploding powers and his history wasn't pristine.

Her father was right. She was too soft-hearted.

Frustrated with herself, she rolled off Raj. He gave a light sigh and didn't move to get up.

She stood and shook out her dress, futilely trying to smooth away some of the wrinkles. It was covered in the weird gel that coated the room.

"Anybody hurt?" Cannon's voice echoed in the empty room. Their footsteps squished into the slime, they moved sluggishly through it. Arif exclaimed over a lost shoe, then dug, wrist deep, to get it out of the muck.

Kaina looked around, confused. "I don't understand. Where are we?" She was huddled on the ground. Violet had her arms around the little girl.

This was Kaina's fault.

"Why'd you push me?" Lace exclaimed. Her voice sounded loud.

Kaina's face went completely blank, and Violet looked confused. "What do you mean?" Violet asked.

"She pushed me into the hallway." Lace took a step towards the child, frowning. "Or else I never would've moved. And now this!"

Kaina trembled all over. "I didn't push her." She spoke

to the group in a small voice.

Oh great, now everyone was looking at her as if she had just slapped the child. Kaina looked down and her hair fell in front of her face like a curtain. The group piped up to excuse the girl.

"Maybe she tripped?" Arif said.

"Why would she push you?" Violet asked.

"She's just a scared child," Delia said.

"No need to worry about it," Cannon said. "It's all in the past."

It was in the past, but there was something off about that child. And she couldn't keep accusing her without proof. She'd just have to wait and catch her in the act next time.

There were more pressing things to worry about at the moment than a seven year old mystery.

The room was perfectly round and white. Light came from the room itself—glowing from an illumination spell. "It looks like we're inside a glowing egg," Lace said.

Delia's hair had slipped out of its elegant twist. She tried to scrape the goo out, a disgusted look on her face.

It smelled like fresh rain, and the air felt charged—like the weather before a storm. And the smell of decay was strong. The fine black hairs on her arm stood straight on end. Lace swallowed. She had a bad feeling in the pit of her stomach.

"Where are we?" Violet said, clenching the hems of her sleeves nervously.

"It's an illusion." Delia held her hand out, feeling the air, her plump, delicate wrist up.

Lace frowned, trying to repress a shiver. "What? You mean this isn't real?"

Delia shook her head. "This is all a trick. Perhaps even the maze was a trick."

"Strange," Cannon breathed.

Raj still hadn't moved.

"Are you hurt?" She checked him out from the corner of her eye.

"No." He propped himself on his elbows. "I need to figure out who captured us."

"No place good, no place good." Kaina hugged herself and curled into a ball.

Violet knelt beside her and smoothed her hair. One Eye stood above them both, tense as he studied the room.

"We have to get out of here!" Kaina cried.

Lace felt sick. "If we die in an illusion, do we die out of the illusion?" she asked Delia.

"I don't know," Delia whispered. "I could never perform a transformation or illusion like this."

"Why are they doing this?" Violet said.

"Only someone supremely powerful could create an illusion this large," Cannon said. "And take away our magic at the same time."

"Or a *group* of powerful people," Raj said, getting up.

"But why?" Lace echoed Violet.

Raj crossed his arms, pausing before he spoke. "They want to toy with us."

Then everything went dark.

Black.

No, not just black. A void. Lace fell to her knees and drew her knife, panting.

A male voice spoke as if he were right in front of her face. But the voice was new. Not one of the student's. She grit her teeth, trying to hold back her fear.

The voice said, "Kill the impostor, and you'll live."

Chapter Twenty-One
Spirit Sphere

The light abruptly returned. She was in the room, surrounded by the students. Her heart thudded in her ears. Her body felt so strange, for everything seemed real but her mind screamed that it wasn't.

The room was hotter than before. She was on her knees, coated in sweat and slime. Her knife was steady, guarding her body. For the first time she felt imminent danger from people, not from circumstances. "D-d-did anyone else hear that?"

Everybody nodded.

"Who's the impostor?" Arif's voice rang out, sharp and frightened. He backed away from the group, drawing his sword. In the stillness her senses were heightened, and she feared what they'd do to each other.

"We have to calm down and think about this together," Cannon said. "That message might just be sent to separate us. To mess with our minds."

Arif was as far away as he could get, his back against the incline on the other side. He groaned as if in pain and grabbed his hair, saying something quietly to himself over and over again.

"I bet someone here controls our magic." Violet looked around at each person. "We catch that person, we catch the impostor."

Delia clenched her jaw and traded a glance with Cannon. "The pirate fights for no one but himself—he's probably here with nefarious purpose."

Violet's eyes widened in anger. "You married King James of one mind, I heard. You pursued *him*. If I had to bet my nose on an impostor, it'd be you."

The light flickered like lightning, and Lace heard a crackle. One Eye glared so fiercely at Delia that she backed close to Cannon. "It's not me," she whispered.

"It's not me! Oh Gods," Arif shouted and punched the wall. It made a squishing sound. "Stuck in a death trap with a bunch of traitors. I never should've left the sea. Why did I think this could work?" He pointed his sword at everyone. "Stay away from me. If you come near, I'll kill you!"

"Watch it, Arif!" Cannon said.

"Calm down," Raj said.

"Why are you so panicked, Pirate?" Delia said. "Unless you have something to hide?"

Lace stepped forward. "No matter what, there's no way I'd kill any one of you," she said. Lace looked to Raj, wondering what he thought about the message. But he said nothing, only studied each of the students.

Shaky from the tension in the room, she bent and adjusted the straps on her shoes. The floor was so sticky she feared her shoes would get sucked off. Dread rose in her. Whatever they were here for, it was a hellish setting for a fight. Close quarters, slimy terrain, and no cover.

"We're in here together," Raj said, his voice resounding through the room. "Controlled by some master puppeteer. Perhaps someone trying to get at Bahir. We need to get out of this together." He doubled over, wincing in pain. "Oh, this room feels strange."

Lace touched his shoulder. "Are you ill?"

Raj shook his head, but his face paled.

One Eye jerked his head up as if something caught his eye. Lace didn't see anything, but Violet winced. "Do you see them?" she asked. One Eye slowly shook his head.

"What is it?" Delia asked.

A fine dust appeared in the room.

"What the . . ." Lace said.

It sparkled in and out of vision, as if from another plane. Lace ran her hand through it, but it didn't waft or wan. This was not real.

She gripped her dagger's hilt even tighter.

Raj choked. He held a hand to his throat, his face growing red.

"What is it, Raj?" She put a hand on his shoulder.

He fell to his knees, heaving. Lace drew his hair back from his forehead. His skin was hot. He gagged, then threw up.

One Eye drew his sword and a long knife, crossing them in an X in front of him. He crept forward, his footsteps squishing on the gooey floor.

Raj coughed, then wiped his lips with his tunic. With a sigh, he sat back. Sweat beaded his forehead.

"What's going on?" Arif said.

"Did a spell do that to you?" Lace asked Raj. Though she didn't have her magic back, she was started to trust her natural instinct better. And it was telling her that he'd just been cursed.

He closed his eyes. "I just need to rest."

Violet was still looking up, though nothing was on the

ceiling that Lace could see. Her hair was disheveled, and one dress strap had slipped off.

Kaina was huddled and unmoving on Violet's lap.

"What do we do about the impostor?" Delia asked Cannon privately, but everyone could hear.

Cannon shrugged, searching for something in his bag. "I don't care. There's not enough evidence to prove anything. Even if there is, I'm not going to kill anyone."

"Killing too good for you, Doctor?" Arif said. "You let others fight for peace, then you'll enjoy it once it's here."

"Killing for peace? Isn't that at odds?" Raj said, his eyes still closed.

Lace flushed. "Zoto's protection of the Eastern Trail brings peace and prosperity to all the Eastern region!"

"There are other ways besides the sword," Cannon said.

"Yes, like arrows and spears," Lace said.

"Like knowledge and development," Cannon said.

"Scad, I'm surrounded by cowards!" Arif said. "And you!" He turned to Raj, whose eyes snapped open at the anger coming his way. "Like you're one to talk—the last Pathfinder."

Raj's face was an immovable wall, letting no emotion come in or out. Arif stalked to him and knelt so they were face to face.

"What'd you do in the King's castle for two years? Huh? He probably released you on purpose, as a spy. Did he set you up nice, line your pockets with gold like he does his—"

Raj interrupted, his voice soft and strong. "He wanted me to summon a star."

Everyone stilled, shocked.

"But that would mean—" Cannon started.

"Immortality," Raj finished.

Delia's hand flew to her mouth, her eyes scared.

"What did you do?" Lace asked.

Raj straightened. "Let the entire world fall under King James' rule for eternity? It wasn't even a question for me. I stood under the torture for two years. The only thing I feared was—" He looked at Lace. "Was that he'd get an illusionist to dig in my mind and control it."

Violet winced. "They can do that?"

Cannon answered. "Yes. Powerful illusionists can control minds."

They were all silent, and Lace knew each person was wondering if that was what was happening to them at that very moment.

"So . . ." Raj rose up so he was only inches from Arif's nose. "All that to say—my pockets were lined with my blood, not his gold, by the time I escaped the dungeon."

And he had the scars to prove it. She'd seen them in the courtyard.

"That still doesn't explain the massacre of everyone in your sect, except you," Arif said stubbornly.

"Who do you think is the impostor?" Delia asked Cannon.

The lights flickered again. Something felt like it brushed her leg, but when she looked down nothing was there. Her stomach dropped. Was she imagining it?

One Eye still had not relaxed. His swords were drawn. He suddenly ducked and darted to the side.

Lace couldn't see anything.

He crouched low to the ground. The room was silent and charged.

Violet whispered in a sing-song voice, "One Eye has his magic back."

A rattle sounded right in Lace's ear. She swiped and moved, trying to get away. It was sharper and higher than anything she'd ever heard.

A bug scuttled over her sandaled foot and she kicked. Then another was on her other foot, and she felt one crawl up her arm.

Lace jerked, brushing it off. Dozens of bugs crawled up her legs. She bit back a scream. Lifting her skirts, she shook them out and stomped her feet.

But nothing was there. Not one bug.

What was this?

Chapter Twenty-Two
The Infestation

The hairs on her arm stood on end.

Arif hit at something in front of his face. Her skin crackled with electricity, and the air dried out. It smelled like burning paper.

The room darkened and a shadow sucked through the walls, gloaming towards them.

An overwhelming sense of oppression fell over her, as if a dark blanket tried to smother her soul. Her lungs clenched, and she had to force herself to take deep breaths.

Kaina bolted out of Violet's lap, sprinting as fast as she could go. Her skirt tripped her but instead of falling something invisible caught her and propelled her forward. She flew so fast she was almost a blur.

A low groan came from Raj.

"They're here? Are they here?" Violet shouted, twirling around, looking for something. "Do you see them, One Eye?"

The invisible bugs still crawled up Lace's body. She brushed them off, face curled in disgust. "Th-there are b-b-bugs on me!" she said in a trembling voice, scratching her back. "Augh, bugs are all over me!"

Delia covered her mouth, cheeks bulging, and then retched on the ground. Cannon hovered over her, brushing back her hair. Then something invisible grabbed his foot and jerked him to the ceiling. He hung suspended, his hands and feet spread, locked in an immovable binding. Delia screamed. The horrified sound resounded in the small room. Echoed in Lace's ears.

The bugs skittered up her legs. She took a deep breath and held it, forcing down the panic.

Raj reached for her, but his legs wouldn't move no matter how he strained them. Eyes wide, he looked her up and down. "I don't see any bugs on you."

"What's going on?" Arif said in a choked voice. He gripped his neck, eyes wide, veins bulging.

Violet cried out and held her arms above her head, as if keeping something at bay. Her knees buckled. Something was crushing her. "One Eye!"

One Eye, sword flashing, lunged at the air above her. His sword caught, then sliced through something. A monstrous shriek ripped through the room, so loud Lace covered her ears with her hands.

The pressure over Violet disappeared. She leapt up.

One Eye grabbed Violet's wrist and pulled her behind him, backing up, facing the middle of the room.

Raj lowered into a defensive stance. He pulled at his legs, but they were stuck on the floor. Even now, his voice was calm. "Something's trying to possess us. Don't let it inside you. Keep your soul clean."

Lace scanned the empty room.

"Demons," she whispered.

Chapter Twenty-Three

The Demon Fight

The demon bugs were all over her.

Lace's heart hammered in her ears. Her flesh crawled with hundreds of ticklish legs skittering up her arms, across her collarbone, down her neckline, in her ear. She jerked away and hit at them, but they didn't come off. Her chest tightened.

It was not all in her mind, but it was on a different plane. They were real but she couldn't reach them. She couldn't fight them. Gritting her teeth, she tried to calm herself so she could help the others.

Though she didn't trust them, she didn't want them slaughtered by a host of demons, either. "If you have the chance to save someone, do," her parents always told. "No one can see all ends."

Arif grunted and his back arched so far back it might've snapped. Every muscle in his body tensed and a guttural scream tore out of him.

"Somebody help him," she cried.

"I can't move," Raj said. "I'm sinking into the ground!"

Grunting, Raj pulled at his legs as if they were falling into the floor. His muscles were tight and sweat streamed down his face.

"Raj," she said. Something landed on her cheek and she shook it off. He looked up, eyes wide. "You're not sinking."

"Don't let them inside you," Violet said. "Steel your heart against them."

Raj took a shuddering breath, then reached for her. She tried to move to him, but a sharp bite gouged her ankle. Twisting, she hit at it. Then she lost her balance and fell to her knees.

She suddenly felt a bug in her mouth. It was hairy, with long legs.

Lace gagged, coughing and choking. Oh Gods. She couldn't lose it. Before panic overtook her, she closed her eyes and took a deep breath through her nose, centering herself. She guarded her heart from attack and tried to ignore the feeling in her mouth.

The bug disappeared. Then something with pinchers

bored into the soft flesh of her wrist—right into her vein. Blood trickled out a tiny hole. "They're climbing in me!" she squealed.

Raj struggled to break free, angry grunts coming from him.

Her vision swam. Lace bent double and jerked her arms out to stay upright. Another demon bug scratched at her neck, so quick she couldn't reach it. It tore through her delicate skin. She felt it slither down her chest, under her skin. Pain exploded in her heart. Clenching her jaw, she held back a scream.

"Get out," she said through clenched teeth. Gasping, she clutched her chest and took a deep breath. The pain subsided. She glanced around. How were the others faring?

One Eye was the only one who looked in control.

Kaina was running circles so fast she was almost invisible, propelled by an otherworldly source. Her little body looked wrenched in pain.

When she passed One Eye, he held out his sword, right above her head. There was a high-pitched whistle and a *pop*, like something exploded. Kaina staggered sideways, then fell to the ground. Her form was disheveled and her legs trembled. She clutched her side, panting, staying in a fetal position.

One Eye pulled her behind him, where Violet took her in an embrace. “Oh no. Arif!” Violet pointed.

The whites of Arif’s eyes were completely black, as if overtaken by a shadow. Tingles went up Lace’s spine. Whoever this was, it wasn’t Arif anymore. His body tightened as stiff as a tree.

He made for Delia, his sword pointed at her heart.

“Stop!” Cannon shouted from the ceiling.

One Eye ran for Delia, who was still retching. Her lips were blue and she couldn’t catch her breath. Clear fluid poured out of her mouth. He wrapped his fingers around her neck, and, muscles straining, pulled something off.

Delia took a gasping breath and then staggered to her feet. The invisible thing One Eye had peeled off began attacking him.

A bug crawled up Lace’s leg but she shook it off. Arif was almost to One Eye, his void-black eyes like holes in his head. His walk was stiff and painful.

“Arif! Stop!” Raj shouted. But whatever held him wouldn’t let him move

One Eye needed help!

She ran for him, ignoring the bugs crawling around her neck and in her dress.

Arif swung his sword and One Eye ducked, then kicked

him in the chest. Falling to the ground, Arif didn't even blink.

One Eye wrestled with the invisible demon, punching and smashing it into the ground, dropping his long knife. Delia ran for Kaina and Violet, sobbing. One Eye beat the thing over and over. A welt appeared on his neck and he twisted, grunting. Arif wrenched to his feet.

One Eye's hands were trapped at his sides. He strained with all his might but couldn't move.

Lace heard a groan from above. Looking up, she saw Cannon's face was completely blue—something was suffocating him.

Lace drew her sword. "One Eye! Help Cannon!" Bugs crawled down her bodice and squirmed into her cheek, but she tried to ignore them.

The big man was on his knees. When he saw Cannon, he flipped to his back and punched whatever he held in his arm.

Suddenly, Arif lunged at One Eye, sword flashing.

Lace jumped in front, blocking the weapon with her sword. The blow forced her back. She flipped his sword off hers, then attacked. Arif dodged and barely missed her blade. He gave a feral growl, his hollow eyes looking dead.

"Fight back, Arif! This isn't you!"

Arif was somewhere in there and she didn't want to hurt him. She swung again, this time slower, and Arif took another step back. She slowed her blade before it hit him.

Then he convulsed. In a blur of steel and fist, he lunged with his blade. She barely parried it. Before she could defend herself, his fist came up and punched her in the face.

Her cheek exploded in pain. For a second, all she saw was white. Then she gritted her teeth and swung back, jabbing him in the nose. He didn't even flinch.

But he stopped. His shoulder twitched. Perhaps he was fighting the demon inside him. His eyes cleared momentarily . . . then, with a putrid smell of sulfur and a hiss, his eyes blackened again.

One Eye took out a throwing knife and hurled it at the ceiling where Cannon was trapped. It stuck into the wall right beside Cannon's ear. A perfect throw.

The dying demon bellowed so loud the room vibrated. Cannon coughed and sucked in air, his face returning to pink.

A demon bug crawled into Lace's fingers and she almost let go of the knife. She switched hands just as Arif attacked. She leapt back.

"Fight it, Arif!" she said. "Fight the darkness, you bastard."

He lunged at her, severe and strong. She twisted away and kicked his knee.

Why wasn't anyone helping her? She glanced back to see Delia, Violet, and Kaina huddled at the furthest side of the wall. Weaponless.

"His left is weak," Raj called to her, still pulling and straining at the demon that trapped his legs.

Scad. That was her weak side, too.

Another bug crawled in her ear. She swatted at it but it got inside her. A coldness struck her mind. Her blood chilled and she felt something slither inside her. She gagged, bile rising in her throat. Would she turn into a demon soon, too?

"Watch out, Lace!" Raj called.

Arif snarled and sliced his blade through the air twice. She ducked and wove her blade between the strikes. She had to stay focused on defeating him.

Time to attack.

A bug slithered up her neck. Gah!

"Drive him back," Delia called to her.

Easy for her to say.

Biting her lip, Lace swung again. The metal clashed through the room. Getting in a defensive stance, she smashed her blade against his. Then, quick as she could, she stepped forward and attacked. He was fast, blocking everything, but she was just a bit faster. He was on defense now, backing up.

One Eye kept grabbing the throwing knives on his belt and throwing them at Cannon's demons until he was only suspended by his left foot. He covered his head with his hands, preparing for the fall.

Suddenly, a flood of bugs poured over her body. She clenched her eyes shut, but one wriggled over her face and tried to go up her nose. It was the most horrific feeling she'd ever felt.

Hundreds of clingy bug feet digging into her skin.

The little demons flooded every part of her body, voracious, boring into her. It consumed her. She screamed. Scraping her fingernails over her face and arms, she tried to make it stop.

"Watch out," Raj shouted. "Dammit! No! One Eye, help her!"

Unable to hold her knife steady, she turned and ran. Shivers and nausea overcame her. Lace stomped and twirled, trying to get the demons off to no avail. Her hands just passed through them. Blood poured out of tiny holes in her body, and pain shot up and down her arms and legs.

Cannon fell to the ground with a grunt. One Eye rushed to the closest student—Raj. He stabbed next to Raj's legs, and a loud shriek pierced the room.

Lace felt Arif coming at her, ready to cut her down. She was suffocating from bugs and couldn't move. She tried with all her might to fight back the shadow in her.

From the corner of her eye, she saw his blade coming at her face.

Raj lunged and pushed Lace out of the way just as Arif's blade sliced down. One Eye swiped his sword up, clashing with the pirate. The sound reverberated throughout the room.

One Eye was not faster, but he was stronger than Arif. Arif swung wide, which gave One Eye the opportunity to kick him in the chest. He fell, banging his head on the ground and went limp.

Lace's whole body hurt. Raj knelt before her and held her face in his hands, breathing deeply, "It's not real, it's not real," he said. "You're going to be fine." His face twitched, as if he too felt the demon bugs.

Tears ran unbidden down her cheeks. She couldn't slow her breaths.

Raj held her gaze. She focused on his eyes—his green eyes, so clear amidst the awful infestation. He stroked her cheek, and she felt that touch instead of bugs.

One Eye placed his hand on her head and gently pulled

her face up to meet his eyes. He studied her as if searching for something. Lace shook and trembled. The horrible feeling spread until she didn't know if she could take it anymore.

His hand flashed to pick something off her sleeve, and he then squished it between his fingers. There was an exploding sound.

All the bugs disappeared.

She took a shaky breath, then tried to stand. She nearly collapsed. Raj grabbed her. Lace touched her face and arms, but there were no wounds. She heard relieved sighs behind her.

"You did it, One Eye," Lace said. Looking into his one good eye, she saw his gaze soften. "Thank you."

He nodded, panting, and gave a little smile. Sweat slid down his cheek and into his beard. Raj laughed, and the sound echoed around the room. Lace's shoulders relaxed. She sheathed her knife.

Violet screamed. "Look out!"

A sword plunged through One Eye's heart.

Chapter Twenty-Four

The Death

Arif stabbed One Eye. He twisted the sword through his heart with a wicked grin. One Eye arched his back, his arms splayed out in shock and pain. With a low chuckle, Arif wrenched the blade out.

Lace dodged past One Eye and punched Arif in the face. He ducked in time and she barely hit his temple. The slippery ground gave her no ability to change momentum. Her correction was too slow, and he hauled back and slugged her in the cheek. But she barely felt it.

An unfathomable rage threatened to swallow her. It was as if everything slowed. Her senses heightened. The great weight of violence clung to her like the slime clung to the ground.

His eyes bored into hers—pure black, pure darkness.

Nothing of Arif in them, only demon.

She took a defensive stance: bent knees, straight back, arms covering her chest. Using the power from her core, she hit back with a right hook and left jab. Knuckles to nose. Blood poured out of his nostrils and he blinked, stunned.

The sound of Violet sobbing and Raj drawing his sword nearby registered, but Lace couldn't slow down.

She kicked the sword out of Arif's hand. It flew through the air. With a deep-throated growl, he clawed at her. She dodged and kicked his hand midair. One of his fingers snapped. He raised his fist, but she was faster. She hooked her leg around his and elbowed his neck with all her might. He fell flat on his back, choking for air.

Time to finish this.

She straddled him and laid it on thick, blow after blow, his flesh molding under her knuckles, until he fell senseless. His body sank into the white gel, and his breathing grew shallow.

She had to stop herself from beating him even after he was out.

Arif was no longer a threat.

Her hands burst with pain, but the adrenaline coursing through her dulled it. She stood and turned, panting and bloody, eyebrows creased in sorrow.

Arif moved.

Lace tensed, but Raj stepped between her and Arif, his sword raised.

The young man jerked and shuddered so hard his teeth chattered. He writhed on the ground. Slime splattered them. His neck snapped back and forth and his chest trembled. Blood poured out his nose and he gasped in pain.

Then he went still.

Surely One Eye wouldn't . . . die. He was too strong to die.

The big man lay on his back. His breath rasped in his throat, and a puddle of blood formed under him, mixing with the white muck. He stared at Violet, his eyes lit with a tender love. Violet squeezed his hand tightly, her face wrinkled in horror.

Already his cheeks were as white as snow. His life was draining.

Everyone circled around, eyes sad. Lace's chest ached. She'd barely known him, but she knew in her heart he was good. Why did the good warriors all have to end like this? Why did this happen over and over again? It wrung her heart. She blinked and clenched her jaw, trying to stop the tears.

Arif groaned slowly, then opened his eyes, now his

normal warm chocolate brown. The demon was gone.

"Wh-what happened?" Arif asked, wincing. He craned his neck to see the scene. He saw the hole in One Eye's chest and he paled. Emotions clouded his expression. "NO!" he spoke in a strangled voice. "No! Gods, no! I can't. I didn't . . . Gods, no!"

He started to shudder uncontrollably.

Violet's sobs filled the room.

Raj turned his back to the scene and walked to the other end of the room. She might've thought it cold of him, but she felt his anguish so clearly. It was too much. His shoulders bowed.

Violet sobbed on One Eye's chest, then kissed his cheeks feverishly. "Don't do this. Don't leave me. Not you. You can't die, not you. Get up! You've been through scads worse. You're all there is and you can handle anything and-and-and—" She broke down in sobs, kissing and caressing his face. He pressed a weak hand over her head and stroked her hair.

"Can somebody save him?" Arif got up, staggering, looking around wildly. "Somebody! Do something!"

All the breath left One Eye's body. His hand collapsed, hitting the floor. Violet grabbed it.

"NO!" Arif said.

Violet screamed in between her sobs. "Come back! Come back!"

The room echoed with her heart-wrenching cries.

Lace bowed her head and swallowed. Her throat clenched. "He saved us all," she said. "His soul will be honored."

It wasn't enough. Her words felt so hollow.

"WAIT!" Cannon shouted, eyes wide. Everyone turned to him, startled. "Move, Violet. Move. Now. I have it back!" His voice was raspy, as if he didn't believe it himself.

She leaned back, tear-stained and red-faced. He nearly knocked her over in his haste to One Eye's side.

Cannon rubbed his hands together, closing his eyes. Lace could tell he was reaching deep within himself. Violet leaned forward. There was a blend of hope and fear on her face.

A silver glow emanated from Cannon's hands, sending out pulses of heat. He whispered words under his breath and the light brightened. The light threaded into slivers and wove into elaborate braids and runes and patterns. It was beautiful.

After taking a deep breath, he pressed his hands, and the light, into One Eye's wound. It soaked in.

But the wound still seeped blood, and the flesh remained

torn.

Violet put her hand over Cannon's fingers.

Everyone waited with bated breath.

Cannon kept whispering, pouring magical energy into One Eye. Arif gripped his hair in his hands.

How could Cannon heal someone already dead? That was impossible. Wasn't it? The man kept his eyes closed, concentrating on the healing. Even his golden hair seemed to glow from the light pouring from his hands. Each second ticked by, charged with anticipation.

"His heart!" Violet exclaimed. "I can feel his heart."

One Eye took a breath.

Violet gasped, cradling his face in her hands. He took another breath, this one stronger, and some color returned to his face.

"He's alive," Arif said, sighing in relief. "Oh Gods, oh Gods. Thank you." He fell to his knees.

One Eye shifted and got up on his elbow, but Violet gently pushed him back down. "Don't move, you silly ass." She wiped the tears from her eyes. "You need to rest. You just came back from the dead."

Cannon moved his hands and the wound was gone—nothing left but bloody torn clothes over pink clear skin.

"Not dead," Cannon said. "I can't do anything with a

corpse. But he was on the verge. My magic was given back just in time." He clenched and unclenched his fist. "But now it's gone again." He glanced at Lace. "I won't be able to heal anyone else."

"Thank you, thank you, thank you," Violet whispered, never taking her eyes off One Eye. His breath was still raspy, but the vitality had returned to his body.

Lace slumped to her knees in relief. Everything ached except for her cheek and hand—those throbbed with fiery pain.

It smelled like sweaty bodies and egg yolk. The room was too humid. She kept her eyes closed and collected herself. *Breathe in. Breathe out. Breathe in. Breathe out.* Three breaths. Four breaths.

It was all she needed to feel like herself again.

She'd caught her breath but her muscles still trembled from the exertion. Though she always trained hard at home she'd never been on an eight-hour flight followed by a few battles to the death. This was stretching her. And it wasn't over yet.

Chapter Twenty-Five
For Us?

Cannon shook out his hands and stood. "We need to find One Eye some water and food. His strength is gone."

"I don't see a well anywhere," Delia said. She was braiding her thick golden hair in a long plait down her back. A wave of dislike came over Lace.

Lace found Raj's concerned green eyes on her. "Is your cheek okay?" he asked. He reached to touch it but she stepped away.

After this, there was no way she would get close to any of them. Though in her heart she longed to let him engulf her in his arms, in her mind she told herself they were still strangers. There was an impostor among them. *He* might even be the impostor. She had to focus on the task so she could get out and get home.

"I'm fine." She took a few more steps away from him and didn't look back, fearing his expression would draw her to him.

Arif touched his face tenderly, then winced. One of his eyes was swollen shut, his cheek had a nasty gash, and his nose was still bleeding. She'd worked him over pretty good. She gave him the handkerchief that Raj had given to her. He pressed it to his nostril and leaned his head back, stemming the blood flow.

"What happened?" Arif's voice sounded funny with his nose plugged. "Everything went black."

"You stabbed One Eye. And you tried to cut me up," Lace said, lifting her chin. "But you're no match for me, even when possessed."

Shame flooded Arif's expression, which he quickly hid. "You'd be beat if I *wasn't* possessed."

Raj looked from her to Arif with a glimmer of a frown.

"I say we kill the pirate," Delia said. "Before he attacks one of us again."

Violet glared at him. "He's obviously the impostor, and it might set us free."

"No!" Lace protested.

Raj strode swiftly up to Arif. He was on top of him before Arif could move. Everyone watched, tense. Lace didn't know what to do, though her instincts told her to stay out of it.

Raj grabbed the collar of Arif's dressy shirt and shoved a finger in his face. "Cut the lone sailor scad. Decide right this moment if you're with us or against us." Each word was laced with anger. It was the first time Raj had showed his true feelings.

Arif didn't fight back; he let Raj overpower him. "I-I-I swear on Mavriq's beard that I don't intend to hurt—to hurt anyone." His eyes flicked to One Eye. He swallowed. "I'm willing to give up everything to be in the Magic Academy. If you'll still have me."

Raj looked back at One Eye to gauge his thoughts.

One Eye glared at him for a moment, and Arif visibly melted. Then, One Eye made a signal to Violet.

She sighed. "It was the demon's fault. Those demons were *quite, quite, quite* difficult," Violet said emphatically. "I'm surprised more of you weren't possessed. Especially the wee one." She eyed Kaina.

"Let's finish this together." Lace put a restraining hand on Raj's shoulder and pulled him back.

Raj released Arif's collar and smoothed out his tunic. Then he stuck a hand out and helped Arif up. Everyone let out a collective breath.

But she didn't relax. She knew better. They were put in here to be toyed with and then killed off. Everyone had used magic except Violet, Kaina, and herself. Who would be next?

She realized that although she had no magical powers, her natural abilities were growing. If she'd had magic, she'd have flown out of the labyrinth, wouldn't have used hand-to-hand combat, and after the first glance at the student's auras, never would have questioned or tried to understand them better.

It was empowering to realize she was more than just her magic.

But was it enough to keep her alive?

Cannon said what everyone was thinking. "What will try to kill us now?"

"We have to find the impostor or the tests will keep coming," Delia said. "If we kill whoever it is, then we'll be released."

"There might not be an impostor," Cannon said firmly. "It might be a trick to get us to turn on each other. Even if we kill someone we think is a traitor, we're still at the puppet master's mercy."

Those words hit Lace hard. She suddenly felt weak all over, and an overwhelming feeling of doom washed over her. Oh Gods. They were so outmatched. How could they possibly defeat a foe they couldn't even see?

Kaina stood. Her black eyes were stark in her pale face, and the dim light gave her an almost ethereal form. "There is an impostor, I'm sure." Her tiny voice rang out. "And I know who it is."

Lace frowned. Everyone else's face lifted in surprise. "Who?" Arif said.

Kaina pointed at Lace. "It's her. She's working for King James."

Chapter Twenty-Six
The Message

Before anyone could react, the white walls dissolved like sugar in tea.

Lace's foot fell through the floor, sliding through a sand-like substance. It engulfed her shins, her knees, her thighs, in a second. Faster than she could even look around for something to hold onto. The entire room was collapsing.

Kaina was already up to her neck when the entire round room evaporated in a cloud of dust. Lace braced for impact.

***

When she opened her eyes, they were in a dim room with no windows. White dust settled around them, falling like snow. But there was no sign of the egg room. It was as though they had just drifted into this one.

She took a deep breath to keep back the fear, drew her

knife, and looked around. What new devilry were they up against? She moved away from the group. There was no way she knew who to trust anymore.

It was a gigantic room with a strange design. Roughly hewn log columns held up the stone ceiling. Chains and shackles lined the walls. Water splashed somewhere nearby, making the room humid.

A twelve foot ledge was on one side, stuck in the middle of the wall. It led to a mysterious wooden door but there was no way to get up to it.

The room smelled like moss, mud, and animal feces. Rumbles and splashing came from below.

They were in some kind of holding cell.

A growl erupted beneath her, deep-throated and feral, as if it came from a big animal. Several other growls broke out with the sound of splashing and wrestling.

She leaned down and peered through the wooden slats in the floor, squinting with bated breath. Running water from a spring trickled below. The shadows of giant beasts filled the area. Chills went up her spine. This slatted floor suddenly didn't feel very sturdy at all.

"Tree crocodiles," Violet said.

Lace shuddered. They were apt climbers, faster and more agile than river crocs, and had developed a vicious appetite for primates. When Lace was little, her mother had said she better eat her salad or the tree crocs would get her. She'd never left a leaf on the plate.

Delia peered at everyone with a dark expression. One Eye crossed his arms, frowning. Arif clenched and unclenched his fists, shifting from foot to foot as if full of adrenaline.

"So," Raj said, looking around with an open face. He was the only one who seemed calm. And just by looking at him, peace settled over Lace. "Kaina. Is this a lie?"

"Why would a child lie?" Delia said sharply. She looked at Lace with revulsion. "Yellow Landers can never be trusted."

Kaina's face wrinkled in distress. She started crying, tears rolling down her cheeks. "I just want to go home," she said. Cannon put his arm around her, and she put her face in his shirt.

Lace swallowed. She had a good guess who the impostor was, though it made her feel sick to even think about it. There was no way she'd kill a kid, even if it freed everyone.

"It doesn't matter," Cannon said. "We must consider the point moot. Even if we could prove who the impostor is, I won't kill anyone just because a voice says we should. Would you?"

Lace and Raj shook their heads, but everyone else nodded.

"I'd kill a traitor without a thought if it would save us," Arif said. Violet nodded.

Lace thrust her chin out. "Are you going to kill me? Just because—"

"Do you smell that?" Cannon interrupted, looking around.

One Eye burst into a run. He sprinted away, heading for the farthest corner. What the—? His strides ate up the distance. Before Lace saw what prompted his flurry of activity he arrived at the site. Smoke trailed up from the wooden slats. How the hell did a fire start there? One Eye took off his shirt and started slapping the small flame with it.

The explosion shook the room. She covered her eyes right before a heat wave nearly bowled her over. It singed her eyelashes and made her skin constrict. The room went from humidity to oven-hot in one second.

The wall exploded. Fire burst out. Wood splintered and cracked, and the back-section of the floor gave way. A cloud of mist evaporated from the water below, shrouding them in moist heat.

She straightened from her crouch, coughing and squinting through the smoke. Her first thought was One

Eye—he'd been right beside the wall. When she saw him, her heart skipped a beat.

He was on his back, motionless. Oh Gods, was he dead—? Again?

Violet bolted towards him. She kept her forearm over her eyes to shield the smoke.

He shifted, then put his hands over his face. Lace didn't realize she'd been holding her breath until she released it, overcome with relief he was still alive.

Another heat wave hit them.

Though One Eye had been hit by the explosion, his burns weren't his biggest threat. Fire ate up the wooden slats of the floor. He could fall through any second. And if the fall didn't kill him, the crocs certainly would.

But with no way to extinguish the blaze, all would soon join him with the crocodiles unless they got off the wooden floor.

She had to put out the fire.

Lace ran for the burning wall. "Cannon, get Kaina to the ledge," she yelled over her shoulder. Cannon swung Kaina on his back and they took off. Lace didn't wait to see if they made it.

The blaze licked One Eye's feet—he jerked them back. His back was as stiff as a rod, his shoulders seized. Why didn't he get up?

Violet arrived at One Eye's side and knelt, cupping his face in her hands. She said something to him, quiet and stern. The floor beneath her cracked. One Eye still didn't move. They needed to get him away from the fire and the hole. Fast.

A burst of light made Lace wince. Something about this fire was strange. It had normal orange flames, but its movements were stilted. The fire climbed up to the ceiling though nothing fed it but dirt. And the blaze didn't eat up the dry floor as it should—it bumped against it as if something held it back. As if something was protecting One Eye.

Magic was behind it for sure. No doubt if she could see auras it would be glowing purple. Someone was controlling it. And in turn controlling *them.*

Footfalls sounded behind her. She looked over her shoulder to see Raj. He ran with his eyes glued on the fire. She pumped her arms at her sides, pushing off the ground as quick as she could.

Smoke billowed towards them making her lungs tighten and burn. Her sides ached and she wondered how she'd gotten this out of shape? If she got out of this, she swore to herself that she'd start running.

Raj reached them. He squatted and wrapped his arms

around One Eye's chest, frantically hauling him backwards, just as the wooden slats collapsed where he had lain.

"Help me move him," Raj grunted as Lace arrived at his side.

She grabbed One Eye's shoulder and pulled him backwards, away from the fire. His face was wrinkled in agony, and he stared unseeing into Violet's eyes.

Violet kept saying, "You are not at home. We are together. Do not fear. You are not at home . . ." She repeated it like a mantra, her expression earnest. She kept sweeping his hair back and stroking his cheek.

He must be having a panic attack. One Eye was as heavy as a bucket of lead and twice as hard to move. His body was tense and stiff.

Each gripping under his armpit, Lace and Raj scuttled backwards as fast as they could but even with the two of them they couldn't pull the big man very quickly. And the fire was reluctant to let them leave. It lapped at Violet's heels, almost setting her hem on fire.

Heat waves dried out Lace's eyes, and the smoke choked her.

Fierce growls nearly froze Lace's blood. The tree crocs were in a frenzy, terrified of the fire. She exchanged a harried glance with Raj.

"Violet, you've got to wake up One Eye." Lace couldn't hide the fear in her voice.

The slats crumbled and crashed down, splintering on a crocodile's back. The beast scurried back into the water.

Violet leaned in and placed a hand around One Eye's neck. He stared into space, his eyes blank with fear. Then she kissed him on the lips, soft and tender.

He blinked quickly, then looked up, his heart in his eyes.

"That'll do it!" Raj said.

One Eye stood so quickly Lace stumbled. He took Violet's hand and they all raced for the wall.

The fire jumped at their heels, and the entire floor collapsed under it.

Chapter Twenty-Seven

The Ledge

The ledge was at least twelve feet above their heads and made of smooth granite. A wooden door stood in the middle of the ledge, but the wall had no footholds or any other way of reaching the ledge.

On the door was a message in black ink: THROW THE IMPOSTOR THROUGH THE DOOR.

The group gathered under it.

"What a fantastically useless door." Lace's voice trembled in anger.

"We're being herded like a rabbit to a snare," Arif said. "We must fight back."

Violet pointed at the approaching flames. "Want to punch the fire? Be my guest," she yelled.

"We have to get up." Delia craned her neck to see the

top. “But how?”

Smoke billowed around them, crawling up the ceiling like a dark cloud. Kaina started coughing violently, tears streaming down her cheeks.

Raj knelt and jerked on the floor slats, perhaps to use them as an extension.

Delia measured the distance with her eyes. “If Cannon gets on One Eye’s shoulders they’d be tall enough to—”

“Don’t think so,” Cannon said. “Not without help at the top.”

“Then how do we get up there?” Delia pounded the wall with her small fist.

A roar resounded so loudly it vibrated the floor they stood on.

“Hurry! We’ve got to hurry!” Arif searched the room for an answer, eyes wide.

Kaina was crying into her shawl, loud wails and sobs which did nothing to elicit sympathy in Lace—wait, her shawl!

Lace rushed to Kaina and snatched the shawl from her shoulders. The little girl gasped. “I’ll take this.” Lace pulled on the shawl with both hands to test its strength. It was made of thin lamb’s wool, but would have to do. The girl’s face turned an impossible shade of red. “My shawl,” she sputtered.

One thing at a time.

Kaina started crying harder. If that were possible.

Now, who did she trust the most?

She ran straight to Raj and placed a hand on his shoulder. His arm automatically circled her waist. "Raj, you have to throw me up there."

He looked up at the ledge. "What will you hold onto?"

Another heat wave blasted them and a section of the floor crashed into the river. Lace's heart sped up.

"I'll grab the doorknob," she said. "Now throw me."

Then Arif was at her other side, cupping his hands to make a saddle. She placed a hand on each of their shoulders. "Think light," he said.

She wrapped the scarf around her neck and stepped into their hands. They lifted her as they would a child, their touch gentle. "Don't go easy," she said. "Launch me as high as you can. I'm used to flying. Now!"

She locked eyes on the door.

Their muscles tensed and they threw her into the air. She shot up so fast her stomach dropped and for a second she flew, surrounded by the void. Air rushed through her hair and her heart leaped at the speed. She felt safe.

The knob came closer—eye level. This was it. No room

for mistakes. She grabbed it and hung on, catching herself.

As she scrambled for a foothold one of her hands slipped. Someone gasped. She jerked her arm out to regain balance, clinging to the slippery knob. She barely hung on by one hand.

With a grunt, Lace pulled herself up and slammed her knee on the ledge. "Got it!"

"Hurry up!" Arif cried.

The ledge had looked narrow from below, but it was at least a foot wide—plenty of room for everyone. She breathed a sigh of relief and stood, turning to the door.

It was locked. But they'd worry about that later. The group had to get off the floor and out of the fire's reach. Sounds of splintering wood and growling crocs filled the air.

The smoke was so dense. Her eyes stung and her lungs felt full of the acrid poison. Coughing erupted from below.

They were running out of time.

Lace wrapped the scarf around her hand. She doubted it would carry much weight. Scad! How would they get the men up?

She threw the scarf down, and Cannon lifted Kaina on his shoulders. Her face warped in terror, but she reached out and clung to the fabric. With care, Lace pulled her up. To Lace's adrenaline-fueled muscles it felt like she weighed nothing at all

Lace pulled Kaina up on the ledge. “Get down,” Lace said. Kaina collapsed, huddling as close to the wall as she could.

“The fire’s stopped,” Raj said.

Glancing at the flames, Lace saw he was right. What the hell?

The fire was paused in the middle of the room. The river rushed under it, thick with mud and charred debris and reptiles. The fire just wavered there, waiting. Her stomach flipped.

A magical fire was far more frightening than a natural one. Who’s to say it wouldn’t erupt on the ledge? Or over her head? It gave her a helpless empty feeling. Nothing was safe.

At least the ledge didn’t have crocs.

Lace threw the scarf down and Delia, who was lifted up by Cannon, caught it. She was much heavier than Kaina and Lace had to do most of the work pulling her up. Lace gritted her teeth and leaned back, pulling handful after handful until she thought her biceps would burst. Finally, she was high enough to reach.

Delia trembled so hard she couldn’t grip the ledge so Lace held her wrist and hauled her over the ledge. Without so much as a thank you or even a glance Lace’s way, Delia crawled to Kaina and put her arms around her, sheltering her. Lace threw down the scarf again. She did *not* like that woman.

Three down, five to go.

Violet was strong enough to climb the shawl herself. She was on the ledge before Lace had even gotten a firm grip on the scarf. Violet grabbed Lace's waist to steady herself and they looked over the ledge at the men. "Now what?" Violet said.

"Arif might be light enough to use the scarf. He's the smallest of them," Lace said.

"Especially if you tie it to the doorknob," Delia suggested.

That was a good idea. Without hesitation, Lace used one of the sailor knots she knew to bind the scarf to the sturdy knob, then she threw the scarf down the wall.

One Eye got on his knees, making a saddle with his hands. Arif stepped on it, then onto his shoulders. He gripped the scarf and climbed up.

"The fire's moving again," Raj said. He exchanged an urgent look with Lace.

Arif was halfway up before they heard the rip. A second later he fell, landing on his back, half of the scarf in his hand. Taking the shawl, he threw it across the room in a fit of anger. He cursed hotly, the words coming from the bottom of his heart.

Cannon climbed on One Eye's wide shoulders but he wasn't close enough to the ledge to grab it even if he jumped. Violet and Lace reached for him, but he was too far down. One Eye widened his stance and lifted his arms straight above his head. Damn, he was strong.

Cannon climbed on the raised arms. There! That was enough for Lace and Violet to lean down and grab him.

When Cannon gripped Lace's forearms, he almost jerked her over. She grunted and leaned back, straining with all her might. He swung his knee up to the ledge, and Lace sat back on her heels, panting.

Smoke nearly seized up her lungs, they spasmed painfully.

"Oh God, oh God, oh God," Violet said, staring into the fire. "One Eye!"

Raj squatted and gripped a wooden slat, trying again to jerk it out. It didn't even budge. The fire had almost reached them. Its hungry flames crackled and snapped, consuming the dry wood.

Arif quickly scrambled up One Eye's shoulders and onto his hands like a monkey. He bent his knees, then leaped into the air. For a second, it was as if he flew. His fingers gripped the ledge and he was up beside her in a second. He bounced up and down on the balls of his feet, radiating nervous energy.

"Wow," she said. "Couldn't you have done that earlier?"

He knelt beside her to look down. "I wasn't excited enough then."

"Six up, two to go," Cannon said.

"This won't end well," Delia said from behind them, glancing at Violet.

Violet pressed her hands over her mouth, horrified.

Raj and One Eye grasped a wooden slat and yanked it at the same time, but it still wouldn't move. The men looked at each other squarely. Raj ran to the wall and said, "You go up first."

No! They needed something stronger than a shawl. Some kind of rope? A belt? A—she pressed her lips together.

"We can't let them die," she said. Suddenly, it dawned on her. "Our clothes!" she cried.

Bending at the waist, she wiggled out of her dress. Violet took the hem and helped her tug it over her head. Now all she had on beneath was the linen cloth wrapped around her chest, and bloomers.

Though light, the dress was made of finely woven cotton and two layers of sheer silk. It might be enough to get the men up.

"Go!" Raj shouted, already in position to lift One Eye up. "I'll be right behind you."

"Come! One Eye!" Violet reached for him, longing. His face was red and charred, his clothes singed black. The expression on his face clearly showed his dilemma. What if his action sentenced Raj to death?

The fire was three slats away and moving fast.

"Come," Violet whispered to him.

One Eye climbed onto Raj's shoulders. Damn, Raj was strong. Lace got on her stomach and Violet gripped her legs, lowering her down. Cannon knelt, stance wide, and gripped Lace as well. Once One Eye grabbed the dress, they clung to it. At One Eye's grip, Lace's fingers hurt from the pressure and she felt like her arms would pop out of joint.

He climbed the rope in two handholds and grasped Cannon's arm. Cannon lurched forward, but Arif grabbed him and held him back, pulling with all his strength.

Fear made Lace's heart race. His face was red and glistening with sweat, his hair wet, his muscles pumped from the heat. But his eyes were as calm as a meadow—their light green pierced through Lace. Oh no. Hell no. He was about to sacrifice himself.

"Take care of Lace," he shouted up. "Protect her for me!"

"Not a chance!" Lace yelled back at him.

The second One Eye planted his knee on the ledge, Lace flung the dress back down and almost toppled over herself.

"Lower me down!" she shouted, reaching for Raj.

Raj's face was tranquil. The floor behind him collapsed but he didn't panic. His inner peace shone on his face. He gave her a soft smile.

"No!" Lace said. No inner peace. This couldn't be the end. This act of bravery confirmed all that she'd felt about him—no matter his bloody past, no matter his mystery—he was a noble man, willing to give his life for others.

And she had to save him.

Arif grabbed her waist and Cannon took her feet, and they lowered her. She reached for Raj, straining. The flames jumped and lunged, biting with their raging teeth.

"Jump, dammit!" she demanded.

He squatted, his fingers brushing the floor. And then he jumped, straining with all his might for her. He grabbed the dress, but his hands were so slick they slid down the fabric. She groaned as the pressure nearly took her arms off. He wrapped his hand around the fabric and stopped himself.

"Yes!" Cannon said.

Lace tightened every muscle in her body, trying to keep her grip on the dress. Raj kicked off the wall, walking up it.

She heard a rip.

"Don't kick!" she said in a strained voice. "You'll break it."

The fire lapped at Raj's heels. The wood floor cracked and collapsed, falling into the mud.

Now nothing separated Raj from the crocs and the river below. The landing would kill him. Or if it didn't, the crocs would. The monsters gathered at his feet, splashing and growling, crawling over each other. Eyeing him like they couldn't wait to tear him apart.

Raj stilled. He took another step, gentle this time. Pain shot up Lace's arm, and she didn't think she could hold on any longer. Arif was wrapped around her waist. One Eye reached over and grabbed the dress from her, carefully pulling it up as if Raj weighed no more than a doll.

Suddenly, a flame shaped like a hand rose out of the fire. It closed around Raj.

His eyes widened, two piercing green dots in an explosion of orange. He jerked, crying out. His hands lost their grip on the dress. He fell.

The fire wrapped around him like a cocoon. Raj spread his arms, still staring at Lace, his face full of pain. Then Lace lost sight of him in the blaze.

"No!" Lace screamed, reaching.

Violet gasped as her back went ram-rod straight. She tightened her fingers so they resembled claws and muttered a phrase, then flicked something into the water.

The room trembled.

Then a giant vine—as big around as Raj—erupted from the river. It shot up, sprouts, branches, and all, seemingly from nowhere.

Raj was held by the vine.

He was blackened with soot, and burns reddened his cheeks. Lace thought her heart would nearly burst at the sight of him.

With the vine towering over them, Raj let go. He landed gracefully on the ledge, right beside Lace. The smell of fresh spruce overpowered the smell of smoke.

He was filthy, out of breath, and his whole body trembled. His eyebrows were charred, and soot darkened his face and clothes. Lace threw her arms around him, hugging him tightly.

His body was so solid. Warmth enveloped her. For a moment all she felt was the stillness between them, the peace.

Suddenly realizing she was half naked and probably squeezing him to death, she paused. Only to feel that his arms were clinging just as much to her as she was to him.

Chapter Twenty-Eight
The Portal

Arif cleared his throat behind her.

Lace was breathless and embarrassed about her burst of affection. She pulled away, too shy to meet Raj's eyes.

Smoke still choked the ceiling, the magical flames as voracious as ever. There was a horrendous sound of crocodiles clawing their way up the branches.

With a grunt, Violet swept her hands through the air and slammed them down on the ground. The tree swayed, then cracked. The crocs made their way to safety with the snapping of jaws, deep growls, and splashing. The tree's roots clawed free of the ground like fingers. With a tremendous crash, it landed in the river in a flurry of leaves.

Violet stayed on her knees, taking deep breaths. She looked shaky and exhausted. Lace put a hand on her shoulder, wishing she had something to give. If it hadn't been for her gift, Raj would be dead.

"Thank you," Raj said.

"Holy hell, Violet," Arif exclaimed. "A tree! Did you create that?"

"Nothing comes from nothing." She gave a weak smile and patted her dress pocket. "I always carry seeds in my pockets. With my magic I can . . . um, urge them to grow faster." To his questioning gaze, she sighed. "My magic is gone now."

Lace looked around. The ledge was narrow enough and the ground far enough away that it made her head swim. At any moment the fire might return and consume them. She backed so that her shoulder touched the wall.

Just as she did that, the door swung open. Raj leapt out of the way so he wasn't hit by it. He crashed into One Eye, who balanced him and set him upright.

She gasped in fear.

Through the door was solid black, even the light of the room that entered was swallowed up by the eerie darkness. This was a void. Maybe it wasn't space at all, but a portal.

A voice spoke, the same one that had spoken in the demon's room. It came from the abyss but sounded as if the man stood but a step away. His tone was even and controlled.

Cultured. "Put the impostor through the door and you'll live."

"You bastard," Arif shouted.

The voice laughed, gentle and merry. "Choose one."

Lace slapped her hand against the wall. Her chest heaved, and tears smarted in her eyes. She wanted to just toss Kaina through and see if that would get her back home. Zoto for Zoto, right? Nothing should come between her and protecting her country, especially not a teary little girl.

But the same emotional part of her heart was telling her it wasn't even an option. She didn't want to become the same person she was trying to defeat.

"How do we fight this?" Delia said.

"We can't," Cannon said, regret roughening his voice.

Then her whole being lit up in orange.

Lace gasped as magic streamed through her like a warm waterfall. It cascaded over her shoulders and filled her up. Power tingled in her fingertips. She felt cosmic awareness—the air, the stone, the crocs. Magic! It was back!

Raj watched as it happened. "Do you—?" he asked. "Do you have your magic back?"

Lace stared at everyone, finally able to see them for who they were. She was astounded.

Cannon's aura was white and deep. He loved peace and

discipline and order. Delia's aura was all red, bright, and passionate. Arif's was yellow—fun and energy were his prime objectives. Violet's was a deep blue, with royal purple woven in tightly. One Eye was the opposite—his shell was thin but his heart was strong. He was almost as powerfully red as Delia, though he was ten times simpler than she. He was righteous. But Kaina, she was strong. Perhaps the strongest of them all. Her heart looked like a rock, yet it was alive and creative.

Raj's aura was so resplendent her heart nearly broke to see its beauty.

Kaina was not human. Her aura was the combination of spirit and stars, dust and soul. She was older than anyone Lace had ever seen—at least two hundred years old, with a thousand layers of knowledge and power. It was so complex Lace couldn't even begin to understand it.

But she did see something clearly. Kaina was an ability-thief. So this was the impostor.

Kaina's eyes glinted. "She's going to lie," the little girl who was not a girl said. Every ounce of her childishness left. She knew Lace could see her. Her face went still. "Since she's the impostor, we can't trust anything she says. Throw her in the door!"

"Who . . ." Arif started, then stopped. As if he didn't

want to know.

"Who is it?" Delia finished. She jutted her chin out, ready.

Lace knew what she must do.

She turned to the abyss and spoke loudly. "What will you do after the impostor is thrown in?"

Everyone paused, listening.

The voice said, "I will transport everyone else back to Moth Valley."

She clenched her jaw. "What will become of the impostor?"

"He or she will be thrown into the void. I require a sacrifice for transporting you."

Lace's fingers trembled. It was almost too much to take, the pressure of this decision. Kaina was not who she said she claimed, but she was not evil, either.

Then she glanced at Raj. He leaned towards her, intent on her every movement. Oh Gods, she wanted to protect him.

"What is your gift?" Cannon asked.

"I can see your souls," Lace said, looking straight at Raj. "And you are all righteous."

Lace spoke slowly, willing the words out, drawing from her inner strength. "I am the impostor."

"No!" Raj shouted.

"I knew it," Delia said.

Lace would fight whatever she found at the other end of the abyss. This was not her end. She'd come to the academy to test her skills and learn through experience. Time to do just that.

She squared her shoulders and tried not to think about the danger. It felt as if the earth were about to be ripped from her feet.

Kaina's eyes widened. Aura spread her fingers and gathered the air's aura around her. At least she could fly.

"No! Stop her!" Raj shouted, trying to get past Cannon and Delia.

One Eye grabbed her hand, but Lace wrenched it out of his grasp and jumped. She caught the aura around her and pulled up, twisting in the air. A sizzling warmth of magic and the addictive drama of flight overtook her.

A sizzling warmth of magic and the addictive feeling of flight overtook her.

Lace looked one more time at Raj. His green eyes were full of agony. She had to ignore it. This was the right thing to do. This would save them.

She flipped around and dove through the door.

Someone shouted, and she heard a grunt. From the

corner of her eye she saw something. She did a double take and gasped.

Raj had jumped through after her.

The instant her hand touched the darkness, she was sucked in.

Chapter Twenty-Nine
The Void

She couldn't move. She couldn't breathe. Her body was frozen, uncontrollable. Her heart didn't even pound—but she knew she was still alive. She couldn't look back to find Raj.

Panic knifed through her.

Was this the punishment? Frozen in time? This curse was the worst of them all. It was a whispered punishment among magicians—something feared among them when genocidal maniacs were on the loose. A punishment hinted at that she never realized was possible.

Time was gone.

She couldn't feel anything anymore, not even cold. It was like her soul had been cut out of her body. Had it been one minute? Five? Fifty?

Lace started counting to try to gauge how fast time was going by. She got to two-hundred and then stopped.

Was this really the end? Was she to be trapped in the void by a madman? Who would protect her country? What was happening to the other students? Would Raj . . . she couldn't think of him.

Razors of agony ripped through her—she wanted to scream and cry, but her body did nothing. One after another, she summoned very curse she'd ever learned and flung them into the void, but nothing happened.

She was stuck.

To calm herself, she started counting again. The monotony of numbers helped sort her mind out, to untangle it. By the time she got to twenty-five she—

A brilliant light flashed in her eyes—she automatically clenched them shut. She felt a shock of heat, then an explosion of pain. Every cell in her body tingled and constricted.

Then Lace awoke. She jerked up, eyes wide, gasping for breath. Something held her back. She was strapped to a table in a cold stone room. An oil lamp flickered wan light; she winced as her eyes adjusted. Breathing fast, she looked around.

There were seven tables surrounding her. On each of

them was tied a student of the Magic Academy. Arif, Kaina, Violet, One Eye, Cannon, Delia, and Raj. She was on the end, and Raj was right beside her. Their bodies were still and faces peaceful, as if asleep.

"What the scad?" she said, her voice tightening in fear.

"What the scad indeed," said a voice behind her.

Chapter Thirty
Teacher

She craned her neck to see the source of the voice just as Raj jerked and gasped. His eyes wide and urgent, he pulled at his bonds, panting for breath. He searched the room, frantic, his expression wrinkled in distress. And then he saw her.

He breathed easier and relaxed back on the table. His eyes flicked to the man behind her.

"Interesting," the man said, then stepped around her. "You children are most definitely not the impostor I expected. Which," he raised his eyebrows wryly, "makes you impostors, eh?"

He had long white hair pulled back in a ponytail. His eyes and eyebrows were sharp black. He wore a traditional Dram outfit, loose pants and a long tunic, with decorative belts strapped across his chest. Leaning on a staff, he reached out and touched her forearm.

His aura was thrilling to look at.

Raj lunged against his leather straps, and his face turned dark with rage. "Don't touch her!"

"Wait, Raj," Lace said, still staring into the old man's eyes. He was good. Very, very good.

His aura was old yet not solid as most elders were. It was fluid like water, constantly flickering and flowing around him. It glowed in the most beautiful array of iridescent colors. There were even colors she'd never seen.

At the sight of his arcane abilities, she pieced together much of what had gone on in the past day. His raw power amazed her.

"He's beautiful," she whispered. She didn't know how, but she immediately knew who he was. "Bahir?"

He gave a kind smile and nodded, then unstrapped her leather bonds. When she moved, she felt all of the injuries and soreness she had received. So it hadn't been a dream? He touched her shoulder with gentle hands and lifted her to the side of the table where she dangled her feet over the edge. Then he went to the foot of Raj's bed.

The men stared at each other. Lace rubbed her sore wrists and looked at them from the corner of her eye.

The room was cold and had no windows. They were possibly underground. The floor was clean and swept, and there was a bouquet of blue daffodils on a short table in the corner. The tables stood in a line across from a desk with a single ancient book on it. The other wall was covered in rows and rows of bookshelves filled to the brim.

This was more like the Magic Academy she'd imagined.

"I'd like to release you, Raj." Bahir's voice was calm, with a lilting Drammian accent.

Raj strained at his bonds. "Oh, please do." He gave Bahir a loathsome expression.

"Before or after we discuss the recent events?" Bahir said.

Raj cast a quick glance at her. "You need to let us go, you sick bastard. And free the rest of the students."

"What is happening to them?" Lace asked.

Bahir closed his eyes for a brief moment, then opened them and said, "They're exactly where you left them. On the ledge above my portal. Quite safe."

Lace's stomach turned at the thought of the portal. No one should have to go through that.

"I know you don't trust me," Bahir told Raj. "But do you trust Lace?"

Without taking his eyes off Bahir, he said, "Of course."

"Lace," Bahir said. "Am I dangerous?"

"Yes," she said quickly. "But not to us. You are with us. Raj, please. He's full of light."

Raj shook his head in disbelief. "Why did you kidnap us? Why did you want to kill us?"

"Fair questions." Bahir folded his arms across his chest and leaned against the end of Kaina's table. "I kidnapped you so you would not know the way to my safe haven. And I wanted to kill you to find out three things: how far you'd progressed in your arcane knowledge, how well you worked together as a team, and what you were willing to sacrifice in order to save yourself."

His eyes rested on each sleeping form, and then he said quietly, "Everyone passed with high marks. This school will not be in vain."

Lace's heart imperceptibly quickened at his words.

"Who was the impostor?" Raj said.

"It's Kaina," Lace said.

Bahir nodded. "She is an immortal. She's a two-hundred-and-eleven-year-old trapped in a seven-year-old's body."

Lace was repulsed at that. "Does she eat flesh, as they say in the stories?"

Bahir laughed. "*You* eat flesh, Lace."

"I mean, human flesh?"

Bahir shook his head. "Of course not." But his aura split, as if he were lying. "She's the one who can keep your powers from you."

"Did she have to cry that much?" Lace said. "It was annoying."

Bahir laughed. "She wanted to play the part. But from now on she'll be a teacher in the academy. Kaina is one of the finest mages in the world."

"So this was all a test," Lace said. "Though it took place in our minds, our bodies were still effected. Amazing. " She shook her head in awe. She felt reverent fear of this man. For the first time, she believed they could defeat King James, and perhaps without a great sacrifice of lives.

Raj had lost some of his anger, though fear still shone in his aura. "Why now?" he asked. "King James has been reigning for fifteen years. You've escaped from his service for seven. Why build an army against him now?"

"I'd hardly call you an army," Bahir said. "But, this . . ." he walked to the desk and picked up a notebook. "Four weeks ago I received a message going to Seagrove."

Lace knew that town. It bordered Zoto and Dram. It was only twenty miles from their castle. As he said it, Bahir's aura split again. Another lie?

Lace squinted at him, studying his arcane abilities. "Not quite intercepted it, right? Hmm, you read the messenger's mind, did you not?"

"Ah, Princess, you are sharp," Bahir said.

"What did it say?"

"It said their campaign will begin in six months, and their army is to be ready by then." Bahir set the notebook down. "His allies are flooding in from the West, traders and mercenaries alike, and he's captured or bought out all the mages he can find." His face flooded with emotion. "He's collecting an army, the likes of which could flood through the Eastern lands like a tidal wave and wreck destruction wherever it touches."

Lace paled. This was her worst fear realized. They only had six months before all she loved was destroyed. With a sharp breath, she stood. But her legs were weak; they trembled beneath her. She clenched the table. "We must stop him," she and Raj said simultaneously.

"Aye," Bahir said. "We must." He leaned forward. "I have a plan. If you trust me to train you, I promise we will defeat King James and stop this war before it even begins."

Lace's heart swelled at the words. "Yes!"

Raj looked at her, then nodded. "Agreed."

Lace sped around the table and leaned over Raj. "Let's

get you out of these." She unbuckled the straps. On the last strap she lingered, touching the soft skin on his forearm before undoing the leather. His aura instantly lit with yellow—pleasure. The fear disappeared. She smiled softly.

He got off the table and stood beside her.

"I shall wake the others now," Bahir said. "You'll have to help Kaina and me explain what went on."

Lace nodded.

"Your first test is over," Bahir said. "Time for school to begin."

Post-Test Interviews with Bahir

Cannon

Bahir leaned forward on the park bench and watched Cannon put his hands on a broken wing of a bird. When he lifted his hands, the bird was completely healed. He released it and it flew away.

"Your skills are great," Bahir said. Cannon's eyes lit in pleasure. "But they are narrow. You are stuck on the same path. It is time for you to branch out. You must be more than just a healer."

Bahir stood and took out a scimitar from behind the bench. He unsheathed it in one crisp movement. "What do you feel about using one of these?"

Cannon folded his arms across his chest with a frown. "I detest violence."

"As you should." Bahir sheathed the weapon and placed it across Cannon's lap. "Those who live by the sword, die by the sword. But it's time to form your principles into actions and defend the innocent."

Delia

Delia's heart was in her eyes as she looked at Bahir. "I know you were the one who helped Cannon and I finally escape from the palace. I owe you everything."

They were in the library. Bahir brought a steaming teapot and two cups on a tray. They were beautiful and old, hand painted with an elegant design. He started preparing tea the traditional way.

Holding back his sleeve, he scooped some loose tea leaves into the pot. The minty fresh aroma filled the air. He gently swirled it with a spoon.

"I am prepared to be a great help to you," Delia said, barely noticing his task. "I have many allies in the capitol, and my magic is useful in battle. Together we will defeat—"

"I am very disappointed in you, Delia," Bahir said quietly.

Delia paused, stunned.

Bahir lifted the pot and poured the tea in a stream. It landed perfectly in the first cup.

"Wh-wh-why?" she stuttered, hurt. "What have I done? All I want to do is lead our people to freedom."

"You will not lead us," he said, handing her a steaming cup of tea. "You must learn to become a servant."

Then he set the tray of tea in front of her.

Violet

There was a marble statue of a dragon in the library. Shimmery purple scales, fierce eyes, and claws that looked sharp enough to gut an ox.

Bahir invited Violet to sit in a plush chair with her back to the dragon. He poured her some tea and he asked lightly about her stay and if she was comfortable. She replied that she'd never been so happy. She felt safe.

His eyes flickered to the statue behind her.

"What is that behind you, Lady Violet?"

She glanced back. "A dragon."

He set his cup of tea on the table. "Imagine if Lady Delia came in and transformed it into a real one?"

She crossed her legs. "I'd slap her."

He winked. "Quite a few people have wanted to do that recently, I hear." Bahir leaned back. "But would you?

Really?"

The flickering lamplight made shadows on her face. She bit her lip, knowing she was being led into a word trap. "No. I guess I'd fight the dragon first. Or run from it. Or hide, or something."

"If you ran from it, it just might kill someone else. Or eventually kill you."

She stilled.

"Your past is a dragon, my dear. A dangerous dragon."

She instantly shook her head. "No. I cannot. What's in the past is in the past. I can't-I can't go there. Why can't I just move on?"

He leaned forward and touched her forearm. His eyes were gentle, earnest. "This doesn't have to be dealt with today. Nor tomorrow. It will take years."

Violet was on the verge of tears. "But who should have to remember being a slave in the hex? It—"

He interrupted. "I don't mean your days in the hex."

She swallowed.

"I mean your days before you were sold there. Your family. Your home. You have got to face it before it rages and destroys you and all you love."

One Eye

Bahir closed his eyes as the music washed over him. The room filled with the lilting lullabies and poignant ballads of One Eye's flute.

The notes died down. Bahir gave One Eye a bright smile. "You are a wonderful storyteller."

One Eye's crooked smile displayed his pleasure.

Bahir crossed his arms across his chest. "But sir, you can do better."

One Eye's expression dulled.

"In the labyrinth courtyard, you were the first to see the frozen curse I sent at Arif, yet you did not communicate it. If you had told him the moment you saw it, the curse could have been entirely broken. Instead, he had to fight it all night."

One Eye frowned and lifted his palms, as if he couldn't do anything about it.

"Of course you can," Bahir said sharply. "You can figure out other ways to communicate without your voice." He pointed at the flute. "You can use that as your voice."

Arif

Arif approached the huge library fireplace where Bahir waited. A game of billibricks was set out on a luxurious carpet. A roaring fire crackled and snapped and two mugs of warmed mead sat on the hearth.

He threw himself down on the pillows with a contented sigh. "Isn't so bad as I thought, living here." He lay with his hands behind his head and his feet propped up on a pillow.

Bahir eyed him with a smile.

"I know what you're going to say. I really messed up." Arif didn't make eye contact. He spoke quickly as if to get it over with as fast as possible. "I've handled demons before, but those just slid in like warm butter, and then I had no control of what I was doing. It was horrible, killing One Eye and punching Lace like that." Arif rubbed the bristles on his chin. "And all that yelling at everybody. I did a lot of yelling. That wasn't good. But I guess that isn't all . . . I also accused the queen and Raj of being the impostor, when it was your little witch all along."

Bahir just listened with a bemused expression.

"And I guess you'll chide me for my skills—for not

finishing off that curse and then—Gods!—falling asleep and all but I did my best, I swear I did. Oh, and I know I shouldn't have snuggled in Lace's arms like that and taken advantage of her kindness. But she's so beautiful, you know? How can I resist those eyes? But I'm telling you, I won't apologize for what I said about Raj because I can never trust him. So take me out of the Magic Academy if you must." His voice raised and he sat up straight in a fluid motion. "I never liked school much anyway."

Bahir folded his hands in his lap.

"Aren't you going to say something?" Arif asked.

"I like you."

Arif laughed, a quick, nervous sound. "You like me?"

"Yes." Bahir handed him a glass of mead, which he just stared at.

"That's all?"

Bahir nodded.

Arif took a big gulp of the drink. "All right." A smile twitched at his lips. "So I guess I'm really completely in this academy now?"

"Absolutely."

Arif downed the rest of the mug, then put it down on the hearth. It clattered harder than he expected.

Bahir motioned at the billibricks game. "Could I interest

you in a game?"

Arif sniffed in disgust. "No, I don't think so. I hear it takes patience and perseverance. Not my best qualities."

Bahir picked up a brick. "Exactly." He handed the piece to Arif. "I think it's time you learned it."

Raj & Lace

They sat in a circle holding hands. Tense and confused. Bahir, Lace, and Raj.

The master's eyes were closed, and Lace saw in his aura that he was working some complex magic. Probably in their heads.

Lace had seen very little of Raj since their return to Moth Valley the day before last. They were staying in Bahir's secret hideaway in the Moth Valley Mountain, a simple villa with a training ground in the middle of the open courtyard.

Now they were in the library for their first interview. Lace tried to relax, but the mixture of waiting to hear Bahir's assessment and the warmth of Raj's hand in hers made her nerves raw.

Finally Bahir opened his eyes. He looked deeply at both of them, then said in a voice raspy with emotion, "You are both very special. And both crucial to the end of King James' reign." He squeezed their hands. "If you learn how to unite your auras, your power will be unstoppable."

Lace's heart raced. His eyes were on her, but she couldn't look back.

She could never unite her aura with Raj. That was impossible—it'd never been done before. At the thought of letting someone else's aura into hers a chill went down her spine. It'd kill them. Wouldn't it?

"But there's more," Bahir said. "If you don't learn how to unite your auras, the entire Eastern Lands will be destroyed by King James' ruthless army."

So that meant only one thing. She swallowed. "You're going to have to teach me the impossible then," she said to Bahir.

His eyes twinkled. "Welcome to Magic Academy."

About the Author

E.R. Ross is a pen name for a mysterious author who loves writing fantasy.

Contact: superstormproductions@gmail.com

Many thanks to Tee Morris, editor.

34482819R00142

Made in the USA
San Bernardino, CA
30 May 2016